Baby and Toddler Cookbook

Kid-Friendly Recipes to Cook Together, how Raising a Healthy and Happy Eater. A Pediatrician's Guide to Feeding Babies and Toddlers for Little Foodies and cookbook for kids

By

Aron Smith

Copyright © 2019 Aron Smith

All rights reserved.

Dedication

To the little ones. The future.

Legal Notice:

This ebook is copyright protected. This is only for personal use. You cannot amend, distribute, sell, use, quote or paraphrase any part of the content within this ebook without the consent of the author or copyright owner. Legal action will be pursued if this is breached.

Disclaimer Notice:

Please note the information contained within this document is for educational purposes only.

Every attempt has been made to provide accurate, up to date and reliable complete information no warranties of any kind are expressed or implied. Readers acknowledge that the author is not engaging in rendering legal, financial or professional advice.

By reading any document, the reader agrees that under no circumstances are we responsible for any losses, direct or indirect, which are incurred as a result of use of the information contained within this document, including – but not limited to errors, omissions, or inaccuracies.

Table of contents

Introduction 5

Chapter One: Recipes for Babies from 4-6 Months 14

Chapter Two: Recipes For Babies From 8-10 Months 31

Chapter Three: Recipes For Babies At 12 Months 46

Chapter Four: Recipes For Children From 2 Years And Above 61

Chapter Five: Recipes For Children Who Eat Too Little 78

Chapter Six: Recipes For Overweight Children 92

Chapter Seven: Recipes For Children Losing Teeth Or Are Lazy To Chew 106

Chapter Eight: Recipes For Children Who Hate Soups 125

Chapter Nine: Quick Kiddies Recipes 139

Chapter Ten: Kiddies Recipes High in Calcium and Iron 153

Chapter Eleven: Kiddies Recipes High in Vitamins 164

Chapter Twelve: Kiddies Salad Recipes 174

Chapter Thirteen: Kiddies Cookie Recipes. 186

Chapter Fourteen: Kiddies Candy 203

Chapter Fifteen: Kiddies Juices 216

Conclusion 233

Introduction

Babies are the most beautiful and absolutely adorable creatures when they're not crying, getting lost or eating your hair amongst other things. I love babies! Do you love babies? I bet you do or you wouldn't be here.

See, babies are fragile creatures. They need to be watched 24/7 and not because they might break your reading lamp. Being a parent can be frightening, exhausting and completely amazing. From the confusion that is a crying child to jerking awake at 3am when the baby monitor goes off to that beautiful smile that spreads across their face when they see you. Just you.

There is a lot that goes into the development of a child and one of the most important things is feeding them. Healthy feeding. If you love your baby, you will get their journey here kick-started with foods rich in nutrients they need to grow. There's no bad outcome to stuffing your baby with immune boosters and so many nutrients they need to get grounded. Well, not stuffing per se.

Breastfeeding

Right here, I am going to assume you have never heard about breastfeeding before and even if you get the main point of nipple-to-mouth, there are other things about breastfeeding I'd like to point out.

First things first, breast milk tastes absolutely horrible to anyone who isn't a baby, so don't go chugging it because it looks like condensed milk...It. Is. Not.

Breast milk is technically a balanced diet in liquid form. It contains everything a baby will need ; lactose, vitamins, fatty acids, amino acids, minerals and enzymes to mention but a few. All these factors come together to make instant baby food. These nutrients are essential for the development of the baby's brain, digestive system and immune system.

Mommies also benefit from breastfeeding. The risks of breast cancer, ovarian cancer and osteoporosis are considerably lessened with breastfeeding. Seems almost magical, huh?

From the first time you hold your baby in your arms at the hospital to 6 months after, breast milk is the basic food to feed your baby, all things being equal, of course. If you happen to decide to stop breastfeeding before they turn a year old, that's okay as long you feed them foods packed with iron. Baby foods, please. Ha-ha.

Breastfeeding until the baby is a year old is usually advised, but you can choose to continue for a few months after a year. What you shouldn't choose to do is feed your baby cow milk any time before a year. Cow babies are not human babies, so their milk clearly doesn't contain what a human baby needs to properly develop.

If you're exclusively breastfeeding your baby, that is, feeding them nothing but breast milk, you'll need to throw in some vitamin supplements. That's because, as I said, babies are fragile and they are likely to suffer vitamin D deficiency, especially during the winter months. The dose of vitamin D your baby needs will be determined by your pediatrician, I only know so much.

How often do breastfed babies eat?

The big question. How would you know when and how often to breastfeed your baby? I mean, it's easier to just chill until they cry and you know it's time, but what if they don't cry? Or what if they do cry, but it's not about food? It's frustrating enough that they can't talk yet. The joy if they could!

A lot of babies on breast milk eat more times than babies who are not. The range is normally around 1 to 3 hours, but prepare to be a walking burrito for your baby because they should nurse 8 to 13 times a day during the early stages. There are different ways your baby tells you they're ready to eat. Again. For the umpteenth time that day.

Sometimes the signs can be as complex as turning their head from one side to the other, sucking on their fingers or whole hand, sticking out their tongue or something as simple as waking up. Sweet babies, right?

You would've guessed crying, right? Thing is, when a baby cries, it means they've been hungry for a while and mommy didn't pick up their subtle cues, so how about a not-so-subtle one? Feeding a fussy baby can be difficult so I advise you to look out for their subtle signs as much as you can before you get a mean wakeup call.

Also, while breastfeeding, move your baby between breasts at intervals. Say, 10 to 20 minutes per boob. Try not to leave your baby latched onto one breast for anything more than 20 minutes.

How to store breast milk.

Knowing how to store breast milk is very important because of emergency situations. Proper breast milk storage should keep the milk viable for a few hours while outside your breast. At normal room temperature, breast milk can last a few hours, so if you're in a hurry and your baby can't tag along for some reason, squeeze out enough into a feeder and let your nanny, husband or family member do the rest.

You can also store it in the fridge. This lasts longer, say, a few days, but if you want it to last for a month or more, you're going to have to freeze it carefully. There are guidelines for that on the Web so you don't aim for frozen breast milk and get an expired popsicle.

How to properly warm breast milk.

- If it's frozen, leave it in the fridge to thaw out preferably overnight or leave in a bowl of cool water.
- If it's just refrigerated, put it under running water or you could put it in a bowl of warm water. Keep an eye on the temperature by swirling the bottle and squirting a bit of milk on your hand every once in a while.

Side note: Never ever subject any kind of baby milk to microwave heat. This is because microwaves might not heat all the portions of the bottle, causing some of the milk to be too hot for your baby and you wouldn't even know it. Microwaves can also destroy some essential nutrients in the milk and you do want your baby getting the full package, right?

I've yapped on and on about breastfed babies, but what about babies who are not breastfed? There are a lot of reasons why babies don't get breastfed. I'll get right to it:

- **Breast milk insufficiency**

This problem only affects a tiny percentage of women. It is called **true low milk supply**. This is when a woman has lactation failure. Lactation is basically the production of milk by the breasts, so when this process fails, you can guess what happens. Some causes of this can be fixed with certain treatments, but not all problems are fixable for now. The health causes include :

- Hypothyroidism (this is when the thyroids do not or cannot make enough of the thyroid hormone and when this happens, a lot of your bodily functions start to slow down)
- Hypoplastic breasts
- PCOS (Polycystic Ovary Syndrome)
- Breast reduction surgery, mastectomy or any breast surgery in fact.
- Previous radiation exposure to the breasts as treatment for cancer

This is a major issue to nursing mothers because breastfeeding does more than just feed the baby. It helps mother and child bond. It also provides a sense of security and comfort to the child so you can let your baby suckle every once in a while, even if you don't have enough to fill their little bellies. You could always feed them right after. You both need this.

- **Illegal drug abuse**

Street drugs are not good during, after pregnancy or anytime at all. These drugs have more adverse effects than the acclaimed benefits. During lactation, whatever the mother eats surely gets passed on to the baby through the breast milk, so you are technically what you eat. Would you feed your baby petrol? I thought not. Due to their fragile nature, babies are not able to handle the effects of these drugs as well as adults attempt to, so they can develop feeding problems, brain disorders, poor sleeping patterns and growth issues. They could even die.

Apart from the exposure to different infections and developmental disorders, it can affect the mother's ability to properly look after her baby. Changing diapers when high on LSD? You might throw your baby off the balcony and swear you saw wings sprout on their backs. You will lose custody of your child and no mother will want to be separated from her baby.

If you're a former user and you've been clean for a while, please check with your doctor before you go ahead with breastfeeding. You will be tested for drugs, HIV and other things recommended by the doctor. Go through with it, your baby is worth it.

- **Medication**

If you're nursing and you have something as simple as a headache, please don't pop just any pills in your mouth because you will be popping them into your baby's mouth indirectly and they can't handle certain medications or it can even put the brakes on milk production. However, if you absolutely must take drugs that are not compatible with the whole lactation process, you will have to find alternative ways to feed your baby. Don't panic, this is exactly what this book is about... Body food!

Medications that are a no-no during nursing include:
- Chemotherapy medications.
- Antiretrovirals (ARV)
- Medications for seizures
- Some tranquillisers
- Radioactive iodine

- Drugs that help slow breathing and cause drowsiness.

The drugs above are a no during nursing because of the harmful effects on the baby. Other drugs that are a no-no during nursing because they put a damper on milk production include:

- Cold medication
- Sinusitis medication
- Hormonal drugs like birth control
- Any drug that contains pseudoephedrine

- **Infection and Disease**

Nobody can be completely immune to all sorts of diseases, as nobody is a superman. A lot of infections can be treated without any side effects on the baby or breastfeeding. But, there are **some** diseases that get transmitted just fine from mother to child. These are the elite members of the disease division, so it's usually safer to not breastfeed than risk the life of your child for a few spurts of very important milk, especially when there are other options.

Let's meet these elite members, shall we?

1. **HIV (Human immunodeficiency virus):** This highly dangerous virus is the cause of AIDS (Acquired Immunodeficiency Syndrome) and there is no cure yet, which is why it gets a special spot on the round table. This virus is easily transferred from an infected mother to an uninfected child during breastfeeding. As this virus is yet incurable, infected mothers are usually advised to **not** breastfeed, but to make use of standard baby food replacements. However, if there are no available options, exclusive breastfeeding is usually recommended but seeing as there are options scattered across the world and in this book, I don't think anyone should take that risk.
2. **HTLV (Human T-Cell Lymphotropic Virus):** There are two types of this very unfriendly virus. The first one, HTLV 1, causes leukaemia (blood cancer) and lymphoma (lymph cancer). The second one, HTLV 2, causes lung problems and

brain damage. You might not even notice any symptoms with these silent killers but when they are in the picture, they are there to stay. That means there is no cure and because this virus can be transmitted through breast milk, an infected mother should not breastfeed, at least, not directly. Apparently, HTLV 1 can't survive temperatures below - 4°F according to science so you absolutely must freeze your breast milk at that temperature for over 13 hours first, then let it thaw out before you feed your baby.

3. **Tuberculosis:** Tuberculosis is a condition where the lungs are infected by a lot of ugly bacteria and then you start to show symptoms like chest pain, fever, coughing blood and some others. This infection is highly infectious and can be passed through saliva, not breast milk, but an infected mother still shouldn't breastfeed because she can infect her child through sneezing, coughing or even something as basic as touching. During active tuberculosis, an infected mother shouldn't be allowed within any proximity of her uninfected baby unless they're both infected. If that's the case, they should both be isolated and it is completely okay to breastfeed. There are several feeding options for the period of active infection that should be used until two weeks after effective treatment to avoid complications and a very sick baby.

4. **Herpes on the breast:** Herpes is another member of the elite seeing as it has no cure. It is usually passed through skin contact with an actively infected person. So if the mother has herpes lesions on any part of her breast, it is always advised that she does not breastfeed until the virus has run its course and goes back to dormancy. This virus is lethal to babies, so it's safer to opt for alternative methods of feeding during this period.

Why some baby can't breastfeed

Another reason for alternative feeding is the inability of a baby to breastfeed. Yeah, some babies just **can't** breastfeed and I'm not talking about premature babies or babies born with some birth defects like cleft palate and lip and down syndrome. They **can** breastfeed, maybe not immediately or through nipple-to-mouth but with a little help, patience, time and proper care, they will breastfeed eventually. The babies with the inability to breastfeed always come with a rare genetic condition that makes it impossible or almost impossible for them to breastfeed. This is very rare, but not unheard of, so you need to carefully observe your baby and have your baby's doctor on speed dial. Let's take a look at these conditions :

- **Classic galactosemia:** This is a medical condition where the body cannot metabolize galactose. This automatically means babies with this condition can't digest milk because galactose is found in lactose, which is found in breast milk. Babies with classic galactosemia can't and shouldn't take breast milk or anything that contains galactose. Due to their special needs, they will be on instant formula feeding and other foods that have zero traces of galactose until they grow old enough to deal with the adverse effects of their intolerance.
As infants, they're more at risk of vomiting, poor development, jaundice and sometimes, death. This problem has a slightly less dangerous sibling called **Duarte's galactosemia.** In this case, the babies are able to digest a bit of galactose, so breastfeeding is possible but not as often as a baby without Duarte's galactosemia. They will also be put on galactose free foods to make up the bulk of their diet since they won't be wolfing down boob milk. You'll also have to make frequent trips to the doctor to keep an eye on their galactose levels to ensure they stay in the green zone.

- **Phenylketonuria (PKU):** This condition is the inability to metabolize phenylalanine, which is an amino acid, and if the phenylalanine content is left unchecked, it can rise to dangerous levels which in turn, damages the brain. There's phenylalanine in breast milk but not in ridiculous amounts, let's say a tiny bit, but a drop of water a day will eventually make a puddle, am I right? So it's safer to breastfeed, but in small amounts while supplementing with alternative food choices low in phenylalanine. This also requires frequent trips to the doctor for some blood work. You can guess why.

- **Maple syrup urine disease:** This is another amino acid problem. Babies with this condition can't metabolize isoleucine, leucine and valine. You're probably wondering why this condition is named like some fancy kiddies juice. Gist is, when those three amino acid levels start to rise in the blood, the baby's urine starts to smell like maple syrup for some reason. Even their sweat sometimes, so if your baby starts smelling like candy all the time, no it's not the perfume, so please see your doctor. High levels of leucine, valine and isoleucine can cause poor sleeping habits, loss of appetite, seizures, vomiting, coma and even death. Babies with this condition are usually on instant formula foods that are leucine, valine and isoleucine free plus a bit of breast milk here and there while closely monitoring their amino acid levels.

Now that we know that breast milk is usually the go-to for newborns and why it's not an option for certain special reasons, let's go on to look at a few food alternatives I came up with.

Side note: These recipes are not only for babies and mothers who have a problem with breastfeeding. They're absolutely delicious and a good nutritional substitute for the little ones.

Chapter One: Recipes for Babies from 4-6 Months

This is also called stage 1 baby feeding or the weaning stage. It basically means the period when your baby begins the slow, but sure transition to solid foods. This stage usually starts anytime from 4 months to 12 months. Thinly pureed vegetables, fruits and baby cereal are members of the starter pack. You can choose to skip the cereal and just focus on vegetable and fruit puree. Foods in this state are typically runny with a very thin consistency. During this stage, it's wise to avoid allergens because you don't want your 4 month old to have a crisis at lunch. Over time, you can experiment with different kinds of food but for now, that angel has a very tiny tummy and a developing immune system, so it's best to play it as safe as possible.

If you're a new mom and you're probably at a loss for stage 1 recipes, don't sweat it. I have put down a few delicious and healthy recipes your kid will totally love. Take a look:

Sweet Toes

- Prep time: 5 minutes
- Cooking time: 50 minutes
- Serving: 1
- Classification: Main meal
- Age: 4-6 months

INGREDIENTS:

1. Water (⅓ cup)
2. Vanilla extract (½ teaspoon)
3. Sweet potatoes (2)
4. Ground cinnamon (¼ teaspoon)

The cinnamon and vanilla extract are totally optional and are recommended for babies starting at 6 months.

INSTRUCTIONS:

1. Set oven by preheating to 400°F
2. Wash the sweet potatoes and place them on a baking dish lined with some aluminum foil.
3. Put it in the oven and leave to bake for about 40-50 minutes or until the potatoes are totally soft.
4. Remove from oven and leave to cool for a few minutes.
5. When the potatoes are cool enough, remove the skin and dice into fairly large bits.
6. Pour them into the blender along with water, cinnamon and vanilla. Pulse until you get a smooth paste. Feel free to pour in more water until you get the consistency you prefer.
7. Serve in cute baby plates or cupcake tins.

Peachy Keens

Prep time: 5 minutes

Cooking time: 0 minutes

Serving: 3

Classification: Main meal

Age: 4-6 months

INGREDIENTS:

1. Water (½ cup)
2. Ripe peaches (3 small sizes)

INSTRUCTIONS:

1. Slice the peaches into two halves and remove the pit.
2. Put peaches in a pan with the flesh side facing the bottom. Pour some water and let it simmer on medium heat until it's totally soft and easy to peel. This should take around 10 to 13 minutes.
3. Remove it from heat and leave to cool. When it's cool enough to touch or hold, peel the skin and place the skinless peach in a blender with the water it simmered in. Pulse until a smooth paste is formed.
4. Pour the puree into ice trays and freeze until a bit solid then serve with plain yogurt if you like or not!

Sweet Potato Puree

- Prep time: 3 minutes
- Cooking time: 10 minutes
- Serving: 1
- Classification: Main meal
- Age: 4-6 months

INGREDIENTS:

1. Water (¾ cup)
2. Sweet potato (1 small)

INSTRUCTIONS:

1. Remove the skin of the sweet potato and dice the flesh into small chunks.
2. Pour water in a pot and put the sweet potatoes bits in to boil.

3. When it starts to bubble, bring the heat to medium low and let the potatoes simmer for 9 minutes or until it is thoroughly cooked. If it isn't soft enough after 9 minutes, add more water and leave it to simmer for a few more minutes.
4. Put the soft potato chunks through a food processor and puree until it is thoroughly smooth.
5. Let it cool before you serve.

Baby Rice Cereal

- Prep time: 3 minutes
- Cooking time: 0 minutes
- Serving: 1
- Classification: Main meal
- Age: 4-6 months

INGREDIENTS:

1. Water or instant formula milk (⅓ cup)
2. Brown rice cereal (¼ cup)

INSTRUCTIONS:

1. Pour the water or formula milk into a tiny bowl.
2. Stir in the brown rice cereal until it is thick enough or not so thick. Depends on you and your baby.
3. When it is properly mixed, serve in a small baby bowl.

Apple, Pumpkin And Banana Puree

- Prep time: 5 minutes.
- Cooking time: 10 minutes
- Serving: 1
- Classification: Main meal
- Age: 4-6 months

INGREDIENTS:

1. Apple (1 small sized)
2. Water (1 cup)
3. Pumpkin (½ cup)
4. Banana (1 finger)

INTRODUCTIONS:

1. Remove the skin of the pumpkin and dice into bits.
2. Remove the skin of the apple, take out the core and then proceed to dice into bits
3. Remove the skin of the banana and cut into chunks.
4. Throw the pumpkin and apple bits in a pot and add water
5. Once it starts to boil, lower heat to medium low and let it simmer for a bit, say 6 to 10 minutes or until its soft.
6. Now add the banana chunks to the pumpkin and apple mix.
7. Remove it from heat, let it cool for it and then pour everything into a blender. Pulse until you get a very smooth paste.
8. Serve!

Apple And Yogurt Combo

- Prep time: 5 minutes
- Cooking time: 10 minutes
- Serving: 1
- Classification: Main meal
- Age: 4-6 months

INGREDIENTS:

1. Water (half a cup)
2. Apple (1 small size)
3. Full fat yogurt (half a cup)

INSTRUCTIONS:

1. Remove the skin of the apple, take out the core and dice it into bits.
2. Get a small pan, throw in the apple and pour in water and leave it to boil for roughly 10 minutes or until the apple is tender.

3. Turn off the heat and let the apple bits cool for a while. Once that's done, put it through a food processor along with the apple broth. Let it blend until smooth.
4. Mix the apple puree and yogurt in a small bowl and serve cool!

Pear Puree

- Prep time: 3 minutes
- Cooking time: 10 minutes
- Serving: 1
- Classification: Main meal
- Age: 4-6 months

INGREDIENTS:

1. Water (⅓ cup)
2. Pear (1 small size)

INSTRUCTIONS:

1. Peel the skin off the pear, slice in half and take out the core, then dice into bits.
2. Put the pear dices and water in a small pot and put on the heat.
3. Once it boils, lower the heat and leave it to simmer for about 8 minutes or until you stick a fork in the pear bits and find they're very soft.
4. Remove from heat and leave to cool for a few minutes. Once it's cool enough, blend until it's very smooth.
5. Serve in a cute baby bowl or any bowl really.

First Carrots Puree

- Prep time: 5 minutes
- Cook time: 25 minutes
- Serving: 1
- Classification: Main meal
- Age: 4-6 months

INGREDIENTS:

1. Slim carrots (3)
2. Water (1 cup)

INSTRUCTIONS:

1. Wash and scrape the carrots first.
2. Cut each carrot into very tiny bits so it would be easier to blend.
3. Pour the carrot bits into a pot and add water. Let it boil then lower the heat and leave it to simmer for roughly 25 minutes. If your carrots are thicker, you will need a little more than 25 minutes.
4. Remove from heat and leave to cool inside the broth. Once that's done, put it in a blender and pulse until you get a very smooth mixture.
5. Put it in the freezer and serve when the baby is ready to eat.

Banana Puree

- Prep Time: 2 minutes
- Cooking time: 0 minutes
- Serving: 1
- Classification: Main meal
- Age: 4-6 months

INGREDIENTS:

1. Ripe banana (1 finger)

INSTRUCTIONS:

1. Remove the skin of the banana and use a fork to squash it in a bowl.
2. If you're in the first stages of weaning, pour in some milk to give the baby a familiar taste and also make it a bit watery.
3. Serve in a bowl with instant formula or breast milk depending on what your baby is capable of taking.

Peas

- Prep time : 5 minutes
- Cooking time: 15 minutes
- Total time: 2 hours 20 minutes
- Serving: 6
- Classification: Main meal
- Age: 4-6 months

INGREDIENTS:

1. Breast milk or instant formula milk (3 cups)
2. Frozen peas (3 cups)

INSTRUCTIONS:

1. Put a steamer in a pot and pour enough water in the pot to get close to the steamer, but not touch it. Put the pot on heat and when it boils, throw the peas into the steamer and put a lid on the pot. Leave this to steam for 15 minutes or until the peas are very soft.
2. Remove the peas from the steamer and put it in a blender along with the breast milk. Pulse until it's smooth and creamy. If it doesn't get as smooth as you'd like, put it through a sieve to get rid of the really large lumps.

3. Put the mix in a normal bowl or an ice cube tray covered with plastic wrap if you have one and freeze for 2 to 3 hours.
4. When it's completely solid, put the frozen pea cubes in a Ziplock bag and leave in the freezer until ready to be served.
5. When the baby is hungry, just take out about 2 or 3 cubes and microwave until it's melted and warm. Make sure to stir properly.
6. Serve!

Avocado Puree

- Prep time: 5 minutes
- Cooking time: 5 minutes
- Serving: 1
- Classification: Main meal
- Age: 4-6 months

INGREDIENTS:

1. Fresh avocado (1 small size)
2. Breastmilk/ formula milk / water

INSTRUCTIONS:

1. Put the avocado in a blender if you have one and pulse until smooth. If you don't own a blender or food processor, that's fine. Put the avocado in a small bowl and mash it with a fork. That should do the trick!
2. Add the breast milk or formula milk or even water and mix thoroughly.
3. Serve.
4. If you want to preserve, put the mix in an ice cube tray, put a plastic wrap over it and put in the freezer.
5. When ready to serve, transfer it to the fridge to thaw out, preferably overnight. Once it's totally melted, pour in your desired baby milk, mix and serve.

Chapter Two: Recipes For Babies From 8-10 Months

Stage two baby food is the period in a baby's life where they can eat thicker and more textured foods. There are also ingredients they can finally try out, so feel free to put on your chef hat and get to work because these babies can eat better now! Babies at this stage start to practice chewing their own food with zero tongue thrust reflex. This stage usually occurs within 7- 10 months, so you need to stay alert to know when most of the purees have to go.

I have some chunky stage two foods I'd like to share if you're interested. Check them out below:

Oatmeal With Apples

- Prep time: 10 minutes
- Cooking time: 10 minutes
- Serving: 1
- Classification: Main meal
- Age: 8-10 months

INGREDIENTS:

1. Water (1 cup)
2. Apple (1 small size)
3. Old fashioned oats (¼ cup)
4. Ground cinnamon (This is optional)

INSTRUCTIONS:

1. Remove the skin of the apple and slice in half. Take out the core and shred the apple flesh.
2. Get a small pan and throw in the water, oats, shredded apple and cinnamon if you choose to use it.
3. Put the pan on medium heat and let it boil. Once it's clearly boiling, lower the heat and leave to simmer. Stir constantly until the oatmeal gets soft and starts to for a thick mixture.
4. Leave it to cool for a few minutes before you serve. If your baby doesn't have a lot of teeth or can't chew yet, put the oatmeal through a food processor and pulse until it's a smooth paste.
5. To store, put in an airtight container and place in the fridge. Should last 3 days.

Asparagus Risotto

- Prep time: 20 minutes
- Cooking time: 30 minutes
- Serving: 2
- Classification: Main meal
- Age: 8-10 months

INGREDIENTS:

1. Trimmed asparagus spears (8 medium sized)
2. Water (1 ½ cups)
3. Risotto rice (½ cup)
4. Unsalted butter (1 ½ teaspoons)

INSTRUCTIONS:

1. Slice the asparagus spears into little bits and set aside.

2. Get a steaming basket, place it in a pot with boiling water, pour in your asparagus bits and cover the pot. Let this steam until very soft. Should take about 5 minutes.
3. Take out the steamer basket, turn off the heat and save the asparagus broth.
4. Leave the asparagus to cool for a bit before you put it through a food processor. Pulse until it is smooth enough for your baby. If you want a lighter consistency, add some of the asparagus broth. When it's ready, put it in a bowl and set it aside.
5. Get another pot and pour in rice and water. Put it over medium heat and wait until it boils. Once that happens, lower the heat and leave it to simmer for roughly 20 minutes or until the rice is soft enough for your baby.
6. Turn off the heat, transfer the rice to a bowl, cover it and let it cool for 10 minutes.
7. You can lighten the consistency of the risotto with the asparagus broth or some more water.
8. You can serve or put it through a blender if it's not smooth enough for your baby.
9. Add unsalted butter and asparagus puree, leave it to cool and then serve.

To store, put the risotto in a fridge sealed in an airtight container. This should last for three days or a few months if it's frozen.

Baby Guacamole

- Prep time: 10 minutes
- Cooking time: 0 minutes
- Serving: ½
- Classification: Main meal
- Age: 8-10 months

INGREDIENTS:

1. Minced cilantro (1 teaspoon)
2. Avocado (1 small size)
3. Fresh lime juice (¼ teaspoon)
4. Plain whole milk yogurt (1 tablespoon)

INSTRUCTIONS:

1. Slice the avocado in half from the top and remove the pit and skin. Dice it into tiny bits and mash it in a bowl with a fork. You can mash it until it's completely smooth or a bit chunky, it depends on your baby's preference and chewing ability. If you want a really smooth avocado puree, put it through a food processor and blend until it's smooth enough.
2. Pour in the yogurt, minced cilantro and lime into the avocado puree. Mix thoroughly.

3. Serve.

To store, put it in the fridge and drizzle some time over the mixture. Don't stir. This should last a full day.

Homemade Hummus

- Prep time: 10 minutes
- Cooking time: 0 minutes
- Serving: 1 ½
- Classification: Main meal
- Age: 8-10 months

INGREDIENTS:

1. Low sodium cooked chickpeas (1 can)
2. Cold water (½ cup)
3. Lemon
4. Tahini paste (⅓ cup)
5. Garlic (1 clove). This is optional.

INSTRUCTIONS:

1. Throw the chickpeas, a quarter of the cold water, tahini paste, ¼ teaspoon lemon juice and the garlic if you choose to use it.
2. Blend until it's really smooth or until the consistency is good for your baby. If you want a thinner consistency, add some water. It'll get thicker in the fridge anyway.
3. Serve.

To store, put in an airtight container and place in the fridge. This should last 3 days or a few months if frozen.

Coconut Milk Rice Pudding With Blueberry Compote

- Prep time: 20 minutes
- Cook time: 30 minutes
- Serving: 2 cups (pudding) and ⅓ cup (compote)
- Classification: Main meal
- Age: 8-10 months

INGREDIENTS:

1. Coconut milk (1 can)
2. Risotto rice (½ cup)
3. Fresh blueberries (½

INSTRUCTIONS:

1. Stir in the risotto rice, water and ½ coconut milk in a pan.
2. Put it on medium heat and leave it to boil. Once that happens, lower the heat, cover the pan and let it simmer for 20 minutes or so.
3. Turn off the heat and set the pan aside, still covered, for another 10 minutes.
4. Pour the remaining half of the coconut milk and let it cool properly.
5. Now whip out another saucepan. You didn't think I forgot about the blueberries, did you? Throw in your berries and water, leave to simmer for 5 minutes or until they start to burst.
6. Turn of the heat, put the berries in a bowl and use a fork to mash them.
7. Serve the rice pudding with a drizzle of the blueberry compote on top. If the pudding is too thick or your baby can't chew very well, blend it until it's smooth enough before you serve.

To store, put in a fridge in an airtight container. Should last three days or a fewmonths if frozen.

Apple, Chicken And Rice

- Prep time: 10 minutes
- Cooking time: 15 minutes
- Serving: 6
- Classification: Main meal
- Age: 8-10 months

INGREDIENTS:

1. Steamed chicken breast (150 grams)
2. Raisins (½ teaspoon)
3. Cooked brown rice (1 cup)
4. Plain yogurt (½ cup)
5. Water (¼ cup)
6. Apple (1 medium size)

INSTRUCTIONS:

1. Put the raisins in a bowl of water and leave them to soak until they are soft.
2. Cut the chicken breast into tiny baby bite sizes.
3. Remove the skin and core of the apple, then dice into baby bite sizes.
4. Pour the apple bits and some water in a small pan and let it to simmer over medium heat until it softens.
5. Strain the apple and set aside to cool.
6. Get a bowl and mix the cooked rice, cooked chicken, raisins, cooked apples and yogurt, then transfer the mix to a blender and pulse until you get a smooth paste.
7. Serve.

Avocado, Banana and Kiwi Mash

- Prep time: 5 minutes
- Cooking time: 0 minutes
- Serving: 2
- Classification: Main meal
- Age: 8-10 months

INGREDIENTS:

1. Kiwi (1 small size)
2. Banana (1 finger)
3. Avocado (1 small size)

INSTRUCTIONS:

1. Skin the banana and cut into baby bite sizes.
2. Skin the kiwi fruit and cut into baby bite sizes.
3. Slice the avocado in half, remove the large seed and use a spoon to remove the flesh.
4. Mix all the fruits in a small bowl and put them through a food processor and pulse until smooth. If your baby can chew a bit, just mash the fruits with a fork so there are little chunks for them to nibble on.
5. Serve in a bowl.

Baby's Beef Casserole

Prep time: 8 minutes

Cooking time: 60 minutes

Serving: 3

Classification: Main meal

Age: 8-10 months

INGREDIENTS:

1. Onion (1 small size)
2. Potatoes (2 medium size)
3. Lean casserole beef (155 grams)
4. Carrots (2 medium size)
5. Chopped basil leaves (2)
6. Chopped flat-leaf parsley (2 stalks)
7. Dried rosemary (a pinch)

INSTRUCTIONS:

1. Chop the beef into tiny bite sizes.
2. Get a different chopping board and get to cutting your carrots, peeled onions and potatoes into small sizes.
3. Remove the bottom and top ends of the celery and chop into small bits.
4. Pour everything in a pan with enough water to cover the top and leave it to boil over medium high heat.
5. Once it boils, lower the heat, cover the pan and leave to simmer for 60 to 90 minutes or until the beef chunks are soft. Check it every 30 minutes or so to know when you need to add more water.
6. Strain the casserole broth into a bowl and turn off the heat.
7. Put the casserole through a food processor until the texture is right for your baby. Add some casserole broth to thin out the consistency.
8. This can be served with some brown rice if you like or a sprinkle of grated cheese.
9. Enjoy!

Chapter Three: Recipes For Babies At 12 Months

They grow so fast, don't they? Your baby is a year old and now they have a wider range of food options than they did the previous month. They can even enjoy basic family meals because they now have semi-mature digestive systems and a few teeth. They are open to more food options, but not all of them. At this age, they can eat chunkier food, so you don't need to make their meals as smoothly as before. They should be well cooked but not necessarily as pureed as before.

They can start trying to some spices, but in tiny amounts. Eggs are definitely a yes now, same thing goes for meat. Oil can be used with no doubts now unlike before. You now can also add a little cow's milk to the meals when making foods that require it. Only meals, not drinks.

This is a journey so you'll need to pay attention for any allergies on the way and always have your baby's doctor on speed dial. With all that being said, let's take a look at some recipes you can try out.

Tropical Fruit Salad

Prep time: 10 minutes

Cooking time: 0 minutes

Serving: 1

Classification: Main meal

Age: 12 months

INGREDIENTS:

1. Unsweetened coconut shavings (1 tablespoon)
2. Chopped banana (¼ cup)
3. Plain Greek yogurt (3 tablespoons)

4. Chopped kiwi (¼)
5. Chopped mango (¼ cup)

INSTRUCTIONS:

1. Put the coconut shavings in a bowl and stir in the Greek yogurt.
2. Throw in the fruits and mix thoroughly, but gently.

Quinoa, black beans and corn

- Prep time: 20 minutes
- Cooking time: 30 minutes
- Serving: 1 ½
- Classification: Main meal
- Age: 12 months

INGREDIENTS:

1. Quinoa (¼ cup)
2. Water (½ cup)
3. Low sodium black beans (½ can)
4. Olive oil (1 teaspoon)
5. Fresh corn kernels (¼ cup)
6. Crumbled queso fresco (This is optional)

INSTRUCTIONS:

1. Mix the quinoa and water in a pot and leave to boil on high heat. When it boils, lower the heat, cover it and let it simmer until most of the liquid has been absorbed by the quinoa. Should take 20 minutes.
2. Remove from heat and leave to cool for 10 minutes.
3. Meanwhile, you could get busy while you wait for the quinoas to cook. Get a frying pan and drizzle some olive oil onto it. Stir in and mash the corn kernels and beans. When the mix is warm and soft, add it to the quinoa and mix thoroughly.
4. If you like, you can sprinkle on some queso fresco and serve. If not, just serve warm.

To store, place in the fridge. It should last three days.

Lentil And Spinach Stew

- Prep time: 10 minutes
- Cooking time: 45 minutes
- Serving: 2
- Classification: Main meal
- Age: 12 months

INGREDIENTS:

1. Chopped carrot (½ cup)
2. Chopped spinach (1 cup)
3. Olive oil (2 teaspoons)
4. Dried lentils (½ cup)
5. Chicken broth (2 cups)

INSTRUCTIONS:

1. Put the olive oil in a pan to warm it over medium heat.
2. Throw in the carrots and fry for about 10 minutes.
3. Now you're going to pour in the chicken broth and dried lentils. When you do that, increase the heat and let the mix boil before reducing the heat and leaving the mix to simmer for 30 minutes or until the lentils feel soft.
4. Throw in the spinach and stir. Leave to simmer until the leaves are soft. Add more broth if the stew starts getting excessively thick.
5. Leave to cool.
6. If your baby can't chew very well, blend the stew until smooth enough.
7. Serve.

To store, put in an airtight bowl and in the fridge for three days or in the freezer for two months.

Broccoli And Cauliflower Cheese

- Prep time: 10 minutes
- Cooking time: 40 minutes
- Serving: 4
- Classification: Main meal
- Age: 12 months

INGREDIENTS:

1. Chopped cauliflower florets (1 cup).
2. Unsalted butter (1 tablespoon)
3. Whole milk (½ cup)
4. Chopped broccoli florets (1 cup)
5. All-purpose flour (1 tablespoon)
6. Shredded mild white cheddar cheese (½)

INSTRUCTIONS:

1. Prep your oven by preheating to 190°F.
2. Use butter to coat a fairly sized baking dish.
3. Half fill a saucepan with water and put it over high heat. When it's boiling, throw in the cauliflower and broccoli florets. Leave it to boil for another 5 minutes.
4. Turn off the heat. Strain the water and rinse the vegetables in cold water. Put the veggies into the buttered baking dish.
5. Put the same saucepan over medium heat and put in your butter to melt. Stir in flour and leave to bubble for about a minute and slowly stir in the milk. Leave it to simmer for a minute, then add the cheese and stir until its melted and mixed.
6. Add more milk if you want a thinner consistency.
7. Add the cheese mix to the veggies and mix thoroughly.
8. Place the baking dish in the oven and bake for 15 minutes or until it looks brown.
9. Serve cool.

To store, place in an airtight container and refrigerate. It should last three days.

Pasta And Spinach Ricotta

- Prep time: 10 minutes
- Cooking time: 40 minutes
- Serving: 1 ½
- Classification: Main meal
- Age: 12 months

INGREDIENTS:

1. Macaroni (½ cup)
2. Baby spinach (1 cup)
3. Olive oil (1 teaspoon)
4. Grated lemon zest (1 teaspoon)
5. Whole milk ricotta (⅓ cup)

INSTRUCTIONS:

1. Put some water and salt into a pot and let it boil.
2. Put the pasta in salted water and leave to cook until soft. When it's ready, drain most of the water. Save the rest in a bowl and set aside.
3. Warm olive oil in a pan set over medium heat. Throw in the spinach and sauté for two minutes. Take it out to cool and when it's cold enough chop it into baby bite sizes.
4. Put the spinach bits in a bowl and add the lemon zest and ricotta.
5. Stir in the pasta and toss to mix.
6. Serve.

This can be stored for three days in the fridge.

Shepherd Pie

- Prep time: 20 minutes
- Cooking time: 2 hours 18 minutes
- Serving: 2
- Classification: Main meal
- Age: 12 months

INGREDIENTS:

Braised meat:

1. Kosher salt
2. Olive oil (1 tablespoon)
3. Beef stew meat (2lbs)
4. All-purpose flour (¼ cup)
5. Tomato paste (2 tablespoons)
6. Chopped yellow onion (1 small bulb)
7. Chopped celery (2 stalks)
8. Beef broth (3 ½ cups)
9. Chopped carrots (2 sticks)

Shepherd's pie:

1. Petite peas (2 tablespoons)
2. Mashed potatoes (¼)

INSTRUCTIONS:

Braised meat:

1. Prep your oven by preheating to 180°C.
2. Drizzle the olive oil onto a pan that is set over medium high heat to warm it.
3. Sprinkle a little salt on the stew meat and roll it in flour. Remove the excess flour before placing in frying pan to sizzle until both sides turn brown. This should take 10 minutes.
4. Move the meat to a plate to cool.
5. Put the pan back over the heat and lower the heat to medium low. Now throw in the carrots, onions, and celery, stirring until it is soft all over. 8 minutes of frying should do it.
6. Stir in tomato paste, wait a minute, then mix in the broth.
7. Move the stewed meat back to the saucepan that is now clearly filled with veggies and cook for two hours or until the meat is very soft. There might be some fat on the top of the liquid, so remove it with a spoon and throw it away.

Shepherd's pie:

1. Take out a quarter cup of the stew and put it into a bowl. Add the meat, shredded and chopped. Add the peas and stir.
2. Pour this in a bowl and serve cool with the mashed potatoes.

To store, put both mashed potatoes and stew into separate bowls in the fridge. To store for a few months, freeze it.

Tomato And Avocado Scramble

- Prep time: 3 minutes
- Cooking time: 10 minutes
- Serving: 1
- Classification: Main meal
- Age: 12 months

INGREDIENTS:

1. Whole milk (1 teaspoon)
2. Olive oil (1 teaspoon)
3. Egg (1)
4. Diced tomato (2 tablespoons)
5. Diced Avocado flesh (2 tablespoons)

INSTRUCTIONS:

1. Whisk the egg in a bowl.
2. Stir in the tomato and milk.
3. Put a pan over low heat to warm the oil a bit before pouring in the egg mixture.
4. Now add the egg mixture and stir until it is almost totally cooked. Add the avocado bits and stir. Let it cook for another 5 minutes.
5. Serve cool.

Chicken Curry With Green Beans And Zucchini

- Prep time: 10 minutes
- Cooking time: 20 minutes
- Serving: 4
- Classification: Main meal
- Age: 12 months

INGREDIENTS:

1. Diced zucchini (½ small size)
2. Minced garlic (½ clove)
3. Green beans, chopped (⅓ cup)
4. Olive oil (1 teaspoon)
5. Chopped green onion (1 small size)
6. Grated ginger (½ teaspoon)
7. Unsweetened coconut milk (1 cup)
8. Fresh lime juice (1 teaspoon)
9. Boiled, shredded and diced chicken (½ cup)
10. Fresh basil leaves (1 teaspoon)

INSTRUCTIONS:

1. Put the zucchini and chopped green beans in a steaming basket and place the basket in a pot that's about the same size so it fits. Then proceed to add water, set the pan over medium heat, put a lid on and let the vegetables steam for 5 minutes or so.
2. Drain the veggies, rinse in cold water and set aside to cool.
3. Remove the vegetable broth from the pot and put the pot right back on medium heat and drizzle in some oil.
4. Throw in garlic, ginger and onion. Cook and stir gently for two minutes.
5. Now pour in the coconut milk and lower the heat to let it simmer.
6. Leave this mix to cook for 5 minutes.
7. Add the chicken and other veggies, simmer again, but without the lid.
8. Sprinkle in the lime and fresh basil leaves.
9. Serve cool.

To store, put in a fridge. It should last three days.

Chapter Four: Recipes For Children From 2 Years And Above

Kids at this age are in the toddler stage and have definitely outgrown the puree from way back. They are ready to try out major meals. They can chew better, have better digestive systems and can finally drink cow's milk. However, because they are still babies, they must stick to soft foods because they don't really have the teeth for most things and most especially to avoid a choking hazard. Because I'm a total darling, I have some recipes right here for you, so let's look at some adult baby recipes, shall we?

Perfect Buttered Noodles

- Prep time: 5 minutes
- Cooking time: 25 minutes
- Serving: 4
- Classification: Main meal
- Age: 2 years and above

INGREDIENTS:

1. Kosher salt
2. Egg noodles
3. Ground black pepper
4. Butter (4 tablespoons)
5. Grated parmesan (¼ cup)

INSTRUCTIONS:

1. Get a pot filled with salted water and put it to boil. This is to cook the pasta. Put in just enough for your baby.
2. When it is soft enough for your baby, strain the pasta and put it back into the pot.
3. Stir in butter until it's completely melted, then sprinkle on some pepper and salt.
4. Serve in a bowl with sprinkles of grated parmesan.

Taco Cups

- Prep time: 10 minutes
- Cooking time: 30 minutes
- Serving: 12
- Classification: Main meal
- Age: 2 years and above

INGREDIENTS:

1. Tortillas (12)
2. Ground beef (1 lb.)
3. Cooking spray
4. Olive oil (1 tablespoon)
5. Kosher salt
6. Taco seasoning (2 teaspoons)
7. Shredded cheddar cheese (2 cups)
8. Ground pepper
9. Shredded lettuce (1 cup)
10. Chopped tomatoes (1 cup)
11. Sour cream
12. Chopped onions (½ bulb)

INSTRUCTIONS:

1. Prep your oven by preheating to 350°F.
2. Get a muffin pan and coat it with some cooking spray. Don't leave any area uncoated.
3. Cut the tortillas into a circle with a knife or biscuit cutter and put a tortilla inside each muffin pan cup. If it doesn't quite fit, fold the edges. When that's done, set it aside.
4. Place a pan over medium heat to warm the olive oil. When it's warm enough, throw in the chopped onions and sauté for 5 minutes.
5. Now stir in your ground beef and taco seasoning, black pepper and salt. Cook this until the meat is clearly browned. Remove the excess oil.
6. Scoop the beef mix into each tortilla cup and sprinkle with shredded cheese.
7. Let this bake for 10 minutes or when the tortillas look golden brown.
8. For toppings, you will throw in the tomatoes, shredded lettuce and a drizzle of sour cream.

Alphabet Pizza

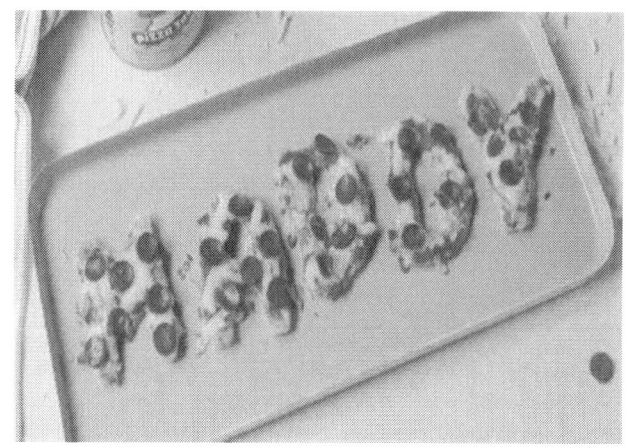

- Prep time: 10 minutes
- Cooking time: 30 minutes
- Serving: 4
- Classification: Main meal
- Age: 2 years and above

INGREDIENTS:

1. Olive oil (2 tablespoons)
2. Pizza sauce (1 ½ cup)
3. Pizza dough
4. Oregano (1.2 teaspoon)
5. Shredded Mozzarella (½ cup)
6. Chopped parsley
7. Mini pepperoni
8. Kosher salt.

INSTRUCTIONS:

1. Prep the oven by preheating to 400°F.
2. Line a fairly big sized baking sheet with parchment paper or aluminum foil.
3. Glaze the pizza dough with olive oil and sprinkle it with oregano and salt .
4. Get any letter cutters of choice and carve out the letters of your baby's name or anything else you'd want to spell.
5. Glaze each letter with pizza sauce and sprinkle with shredded cheese and pepperoni.
6. Put it in the oven to bake until it is golden brown and the cheese is completely melted.
7. Sprinkle with parsley, leave to cool and bon Appetit!

Cheeseburger Cups

- Prep time: 30 minutes
- Cooking time: 21 minutes
- Serving: 6
- Classification: Main meal
- Age: 2 years and above

INGREDIENTS:

1. Burger buns (6)
2. Ground beef (1 lb.)
3. Cooking spray or butter
4. Vegetable oil (1 tablespoon)
5. Kosher salt
6. Chopped onion (1 small size)
7. Ground black pepper
8. Ketchup
9. Pickle chips (12)
10. Quartered cheddar cheese (3 slices)
11. Yellow mustard
12. Sesame seeds

INSTRUCTIONS:

1. Prep oven by preheating to 350°F.
2. Coat a muffin tin with butter or cooking spray.
3. Take a rolling pin over the burger buns to flatten them enough for the child.
4. Now put one half of the burger, the cut side facing up, in the buttered muffin tin.
5. Get a fairly large pan and place it over medium heat. Stir in the onions and let it cook for 5 minutes.
6. Stir in the ground beef using a wooden spoon and try to mash it to bits while stirring. Baby bites, remember?
7. Let the beef cook for roughly 6 minutes before you remove the excess oil. Now sprinkle with salt, garlic powder and pepper. Stir.
8. Spoon some of the beef mixture unto the burger bun halves and crown with a cheddar cheese slice.
9. Let this bake until the burgers are golden and the cheese is completely melted. This should take 10 minutes.
10. Drizzle mustard and ketchup over the buns and crown with a pickle.
11. Sprinkle sesame seeds over the pickle and serve.

Vegetable Soup

- Prep Time: 5 minutes
- Cooking Time: 40 minutes
- Serving: 6
- Classification: Main meal
- Age: 2 years and above

INGREDIENTS:

1. Chopped onion (1 small)
2. Chopped carrots (2 medium sized)
3. Vegetable oil (2 tablespoons)
4. Diced butternut squash (100g)
5. Crushed garlic (1 clove)
6. Sliced celery (2 sticks)
7. Red lentils (100g)
8. Diced sweet potatoes (100g)
9. Water (500ml)
10. Thyme (½ teaspoon)
11. Ground black pepper (½ teaspoon)
12. Vegetable stock
13. Bay leaf (1)
14. Salt (½ teaspoon)

INSTRUCTIONS:

1. Warm the vegetable oil in a skillet.
2. Throw in the crushed garlic, chopped onions and vegetables.
3. Add water and cover the pan. Let it cook for 20 minutes while stirring occasionally.
4. Wash and strain the lentils and throw them in the pan.
5. Add the thyme, pepper, bay leaf and salt.
6. Stir in the vegetable stock and let it simmer for about 15 minutes.
7. Now you're going to transfer the soup to a blender but take out the bay leaf first.
8. Pulse for 2 minutes while adjusting the seasoning.
9. Serve.

Quinoa Salad

- Prep Time: 30 minutes
- Cook Time: 6 minutes
- Serving: 4 portions
- Classification: Main meal
- Age: 2 years and above

INGREDIENTS:

1. Drained sweet corn
2. Chopped cashew nuts (4 tablespoons)
3. Cooked red and white quinoa
4. Diced red pepper (½ bell)
5. Sultanas
6. Sliced spring onions (4)

Dressing:

1. Sugar
2. Balsamic vinegar (2 tablespoons)
3. Olive oil (6 tablespoons)

4. Crushed garlic (½ clove)

INSTRUCTIONS:

1. Tear open the quinoa packet and pour enough in a bowl with some water. Drape a cling film over the top of the bowl and make tiny holes at the top.
2. Put the covered quinoas in the microwave and cook for 6 minutes or until it's soft and fluffy. Set aside to cool.
3. Sprinkle the other ingredients on the quinoa and mix.
4. Combine all the ingredients for the dressing and drizzle over the quinoa.
5. Let it cool in the fridge for 30 minutes.
6. Serve.

Chicken Fajitas

- Prep time: 12 minutes
- Cooking time: 8 minutes
- Serving: 2
- Classification: Main meal
- Age: 2 years and above

INGREDIENTS:

Fajitas:

1. Balsamic vinegar (1 teaspoon)
2. Brown sugar (½ teaspoon)
3. Tomato ketchup (2 teaspoons)
4. Water (1 teaspoon)
5. Tabasco (2 drops). This is optional
6. Strips of chicken breast
7. Dried oregano
8. Sunflower oil (1 teaspoon)
9. Sliced red onion (1 small size)
10. Flour tortillas (2)

11. Sliced red pepper (¼ small size)
12. Mild salsa (2 tablespoons)
13. Sliced yellow pepper (¼ small size)
14. Guacamole (1 tablespoon). This is optional.
15. Sour cream (4 teaspoons)

Mild Salsa:

1. Sliced spring onion (1)
2. Lime juice (1 tablespoon)
3. Sliced tomato (1 large size)
4. Chopped coriander (2 teaspoons)
5. Black pepper powder
6. Salt to taste.

INSTRUCTIONS:

1. Get a small bowl and add the balsamic vinegar, sugar, dried oregano, tomato ketchup, Tabasco and water. Mix mix mix!
2. Warm the sunflower oil in a fairly large skillet and sauté the chicken in it for about 2 minutes.
3. Now stir in the vegetables and keep stirring for another 4 minutes or until the veggies are soft enough and your chicken is thoroughly cooked.
4. Now stir in the ketchup mix. Stir nice and easy for an extra minute. Leave it to cook for 2 minutes before you turn off the heat.
5. For the salsa, throw all the salsa ingredients in a bowl and sprinkle in some salt and pepper.
6. Cover it and store in the fridge until you need to use it. Keep in mind that it can't last for more than two days.
7. Heat tortillas in the microwave for 10 seconds or 20 seconds if you're using a dry pan.
8. Now it's time for the filling! Scoop some fajitas onto the center of the wrap before you add the salsa and sour cream. This is the time to add the guacamoles if you're using them.
9. Roll it nice and slow.
10. Serve.

Chicken Balls With Tomato And Carrot Sauce.

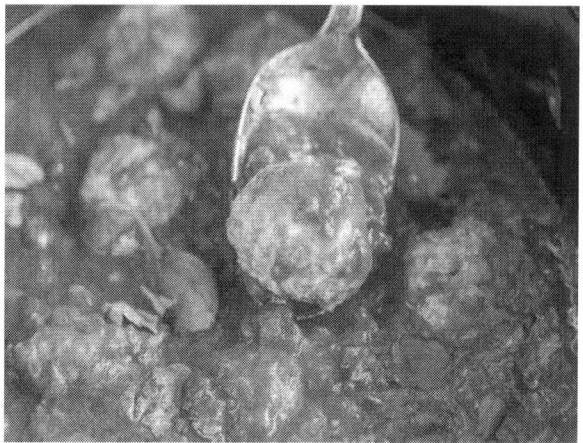

- Prep time: 20 minutes
- Cooking time: 30 minutes
- Serving: 28 balls
- Classification: Main meal
- Age: 2 years and above

INGREDIENTS:

Meatballs:

1. Chopped onions (1 medium size)
2. Chopped sage (1 teaspoon)
3. White sliced bread (1 slice)
4. Grated apple (½ medium size)
5. Chopped thyme leaves (1 teaspoon)
6. Crushed garlic (1 clove)
7. Diced boneless chicken thigh

Sauce:

1. Diced banana (2 shallots)
2. Sliced carrots
3. Olive oil (1 tablespoon)
4. Chicken stock

5. Tomato puree (1 tablespoon)
6. Chopped tomatoes
7. Crushed garlic (1 clove)

INSTRUCTIONS:

1. For the meatballs, take the bread into a dry blender or food processor and blitz until it's in pieces.
2. Now add the chicken thighs. Blitz again. Throw in the onions, crushed garlic, apple, parmesan and herbs. If you'd like to add any other seasonings, this is the time. Blitz until everything is properly mixed.
3. Use your hands to make little balls.
4. For the sauce, warm the oil in a pan and throw in the shallots. Stir fry for about 2 ½ minutes before adding the garlic and carrots and frying for another 2 ½ minutes.
5. Now pour in the stock and tomato puree, leave it to simmer for roughly 20 minutes or until the carrots are soft enough for your child.
6. Now transfer the sauce to a blender and pulse until it's pasty smooth. Pour it back in the pan with the chopped tomatoes and leave it to cook for 10 minutes.
7. Back to our cute little meatballs. Fry them in very little oil, turning at intervals until all sides are golden.
8. Dump them in the sauce and let them simmer for about 6 minutes.
9. You can choose to serve with some rice or not.
10. Enjoy!

Chapter Five: Recipes For Children Who Eat Too Little

Some children eat more than others for various reasons; maybe they're picky eaters or they have an appetite issue. Whatever the reason, it makes sense to force-feed them with any kind of food because it's better to have less calories than no calories, right? Healthy diets for children are focused on providing the right nutrients even with the little food available.. Most children who eat very little tend to be underweight, so healthy foods are a must. Food containing nuts, olives, coconut oil, pasta, meat and other healthy ingredients should be a priority when planning their meals. Let's take a look at some of my combos:

Roasted Root Veggies

- Prep time: 10 minutes
- Cooking time: 30 - 45 minutes
- Serving: 10
- Classification: Main meal
- Age: 12 months and above

INGREDIENTS:

1. Chopped parsnips (2)
2. Chopped skinless sweet potato (1)
3. Chopped golden beetroot (1)
4. Chopped carrots (4)
5. Olive oil (1 tablespoon)
6. Sea salt (¼ teaspoon)
7. Dried thyme (1 teaspoon)

INSTRUCTIONS:

1. Prep your oven by preheating to 400°F.
2. Coat a baking sheet with butter, cooking spray or parchment paper.
3. Arrange the veggies on the baking sheet, then pour olive oil making sure it touches all the chopped vegetables. Throw in some thyme and mix thoroughly with your hands. If your child is older than a year, use the sea salt.
4. Leave this in the oven for 30 minutes while making sure to stir every once in a while. If your veggies are in large chunks, they'll stay in the oven for longer, say an extra 15 minutes. The veggies should be really soft when properly cooked.
5. Leave to cool before you serve.
6. Enjoy!

Rainbow Pepper And Feta Quiche

- Prep time: 10 minutes
- Cooking time: 30 minutes
- Serving: 7
- Classification: Main meal
- Age: 2 years and older

INGREDIENTS:

1. Eggs (4)
2. Whole wheat breadcrumbs (2 tablespoons)
3. Chopped red peppers (¼ cup)
4. Chopped green peppers (¼ cup)

5. Plain Greek yogurt (¼ cup)
6. Chopped thyme (1 teaspoon)
7. Salt
8. Feta crumbles (2 tablespoons)
9. Pepper

INSTRUCTIONS:

1. Prep your oven by preheating to 350°F.
2. Go ahead to blend your peppers 2 to 4 times. You don't want to blend it into a smooth paste, just into bits.
3. Now add the add and eggs and blitz twice.
4. Pour in the breadcrumbs, seasoning, thyme and yogurt. Blitz twice.
5. Now transfer the egg mix into a multipurpose bowl or tray, top with feta crumbs and place the bowl or tray on a baking sheet. Slide sheet into the oven and leave to bake for about 30 minutes or until the top looks brown.
6. Leave to cool for a few minutes before you serve.

Roasted Beet, Orange And Mint

- Prep time: 10 minutes
- Cooking time: 40 minutes
- Serving: 1
- Classification: Main meal
- Age: 2 years and above

INGREDIENTS:

1. Fresh orange (1 small size)
2. Chopped mint (2 leaves)
3. Golden beetroot (1 small size)

INSTRUCTIONS:

1. Preheat your oven to 350°F
2. Wash, strain and wrap the golden beet in foil and put in the oven to bake for 40 minutes. It should be really soft now. Let it cool.
3. Rove the skin and dice into bits.
4. Remove the skin of the orange and cut into bits.
5. Store them separately until you're ready to serve.
6. Mix together in a bowl with a nice sprinkle of the mint leaves and serve.

Tofu Sticks And Peanut Sauce

- Prep time: 40 minutes
- Cooking time: 40 minutes
- Serving: 40
- Classification: Snack
- Age: 2 years and above

INGREDIENTS:

Tofu Sticks:

1. Sesame oil (1 tablespoon)
2. Rice vinegar (2 tablespoons)
3. Firm sprouted tofu
4. Soy sauce (3 tablespoons)
5. Honey (2 tablespoons)
6. Fresh ground ginger (½ teaspoon)
7. Sesame seeds (2 tablespoons)
8. Crushed garlic (½ clove)

Peanut Sauce:

1. Lukewarm water (½ cup)
2. Brown sugar (2 tablespoons)
3. Organic peanut butter (½ cup)
4. Soy sauce (1 tablespoon)
5. Cayenne pepper (this is optional)
6. Fresh lime juice (1 small size)

INSTRUCTIONS:

1. slice the tofu into 3 long bits and lay them on some paper towels, preferably 3.
2. Top the tofu with another stack of paper towels. Like tofu paper sandwich.
3. Now put something heavy, anything at all, on top of the tofu paper sandwich and press. The point is to squeeze a lot of water out of the tofu. The result should be crispy. Press for about 10 minutes and change the towels. Do this until you get a crispy result.
4. After pressing the tofu, put the eggs, soy sauce, garlic, ginger, sesame oil, vinegar and honey in a bowl and whisk.
5. Now prep your oven by preheating to 400°F.
6. Cut the crispy tofu pieces into nugget shapes and place on a pan. Drizzle the marinade over the nuggets ensuring they all sides get coated. Leave this for about 10 minutes to stand then flip and wait another 10 minutes.
7. After 20 minutes of waiting, you can finally put the coated tofu nuggets on a baking sheet and top with sesame seeds.
8. Put it in the oven and leave for 20 minutes. Flip the nuggets so you can bake the other side. 20 minutes for each side.
9. While the tofu bakes, you can pass time by making the peanut butter sauce. Get a bowl, stir in peanut butter and water. Mix until it's really smooth. Now drizzle in soy sauce, add the brown sugar, pepper and fresh lime juice. Whisk until it's all one smooth paste.
10. Serve in a bowl

Oat Cups

- Prep time: 10 minutes
- Cooking time: 30 minutes
- Serving: 6
- Classification: Main meal
- Age: 12 months and above

INGREDIENTS:

1. Cinnamon (1 teaspoon)
2. Smash ripe bananas (2 fingers)
3. Old fashioned oats (3 cups)
4. Salt (½ teaspoon)
5. Baking soda (1 teaspoon)
6. Eggs (2)
7. Vanilla extract (2 teaspoons)
8. Maple syrup (⅓ cup)
9. Desired baby milk (1 cup)
10. Coconut oil (¼ cup)

INSTRUCTIONS:

1. Prep oven by preheating to 350°F.
2. Coat 12 muffin tins with cooking spray or parchment paper.
3. Put a cup of oats in a blender and blitz until you get something that looks a lot like corn flour. Don't overdo it, you'll get a sticky result. Think flour + gum.
4. Pour the oat flour in a bowl and add cinnamon, remaining oats, baking soda and salt. Whisk until it's all mixed up.
5. Get another bowl and throw in the eggs, bananas, milk, vanilla, maple syrup, and coconut oil. Whisk whisk whisk!
6. Add the egg mix to the oat flour mix and mix well. If you want to add anything else, this is the time.
7. Scoop the oat mix into the coated muffin tins and let it bake until the top is browned. 30 minutes max.
8. Let it cool before you serve.

Potato Waffles

- Prep time: 10 minutes
- Cooking time: 15 minutes
- Serving: 12
- Classification: Main meal
- Age: 2 years and above

INGREDIENTS:

1. Quick oats (1 cup)
2. Cinnamon (1 teaspoon)
3. All-purpose flour (1 ½ cups)
4. Eggs (2)
5. Baking powder (3 teaspoons)
6. Whole milk (1 cup)
7. Salt (¼ teaspoon)
8. Butter (3 tablespoons)
9. Sweet potato puree
10. Whole fat yogurt (½ cup)
11. Maple syrup (2 tablespoons)

INSTRUCTIONS:

1. Put all the dry ingredients in a bowl and mix well.
2. Pour the eggs, yogurt, potato puree, milk, oil and brown sugar into the bowl of dry ingredients and whisk. Set this aside and prep your waffle maker. If you want your batter to have a thinner consistency, pour in some milk. Just enough to make it less thick.
3. Coat the insides of the waffle maker with butter and drizzle ⅓ cup of batter onto it. Close the maker and let it cook.
4. When it's ready, put it on a plate and leave it to cool before you serve.
5. Enjoy!

Spring Fling Finger Salad

- Prep time: 5 minutes
- Cooking time:
- Serving: 4
- Classification: Main meal
- Age: 2 years and above

INGREDIENTS:

1. Diced avocado (½)
2. Edamame (⅓ cup)
3. Diced pear (½ small size)
4. Chopped kiwis (2)
5. Fresh lime juice (2 teaspoons)

INSTRUCTIONS:

1. Put the chopped pear, avocado, edamame, and kiwi in a bowl and drizzle the lime over the salad.
2. Mix everything until the lime juice gets everywhere.
3. You can sprinkle on some chia seeds or finely chopped mint leaves before you serve.

Chapter Six: Recipes For Overweight Children

It's easy to assume that obese people just eat way too much. It makes total sense, doesn't it? It's 100% false. Some people can just smell cake and boom! 5 extra pounds. While others can eat 7 times a day, every day of the week and still look toothpick-sized. Working towards a weight loss goal is difficult even for the kids because they really have no idea where to start or what to do and this can result in extreme weight loss measure like throwing up after meals and starvation. As a parent, you need to be present. Take their cute little hand in yours and see them through the journey to a healthier lifestyle. Besides, some kids don't even know or care when they start packing on the pounds. Now that's where you come in. I came up with a list of ways you can help keep their weight in check plus a few added healthy recipes that are absolutely delish. Your kid won't even notice the diet change! However, first things first:

1. **Healthy drinks only:** Most beverages contains an unreasonable amount of sugar. 1 soda can becomes 5 and in no time, you have a baby whale. You need to swap the fizzy drinks and other sugary beverages with flavored seltzers and basic water. Trust me.
2. **When in doubt, go natural:** Fresh fruits, lean beef and fresh veggies should take up a lot of space on the menu. Fast foods and packaged treats should happen once in a while because you can't totally cross them off without having a full on kiddies rebellion. Pack them a healthy lunch box every day because this helps keep an eye on what they eat when they're not home.
3. **Stick to smaller portions:** Please don't stuff your kid with a lot of food, healthy or not. They're kids, they should eat kid-sized food and guess what? They'll still grow.
4. **Healthy grocery shopping:** Think of swapping the chips for popcorn and full fat ice cream for chocolate Italian ices.
5. **Sweets can stay:** If you don't give your kid some sweets, they'll get it elsewhere and you won't even know about it! Save the candy and ice cream for special days so your toddler doesn't feel the need to get sneaky.

6. **Say no to the clean-plate community:** If your child is full, there's absolutely no need to force feed them because 'wasting food is bad'. If they get hungry later, there are a lot of healthy snacks to choose from or you can just hand them an apple. Can't go wrong with an apple.
7. **Daily exercise? Check!:** This shouldn't bet extremely difficult considering how active children usually are. To make it even more fun, participate. You get to burn a few calories yourself!
8. **Show unconditional love:** Being overweight isn't easy. It comes with health complications, bullies, constant criticism, paranoia, esteem issues and other terrible things. Don't add any more to the pile. Support and encourage your child. This will help build confidence and self-esteem while they work on shedding a few pounds and maintaining a healthy weight.
9. Sometimes, all you need to do is ensure they don't put on extra weight. They're still going to get taller and not be obese anymore!
10. **Have your child's doctor on speed dial:** Speaking to your doctor will help you better understand why your child is overweight and how to manage it. Some weight problems are caused by genetic conditions, so now you understand where the doctor comes in.

Now the recipes!!!

Dairy Free Blueberry Muesli

- Prep time: 10 minutes
- Cooking time: 10 minutes
- Serving: 4
- Classification: Main meal
- Age: 2 years and above

INGREDIENTS:

1. Chopped walnuts (½ cup)
2. Cinnamon powder (2 teaspoons)
3. Rolled oats (1 ½ cup)
4. Brown sugar (3 tablespoons)
5. Chopped dried apples (½ cup)
6. Wild blueberries (2 cups)
7. Fresh apple juice

INSTRUCTIONS:

1. Prep oven by preheating to 160°C
2. Get a bowl and pour in sugar, oats and cinnamon. Mix totally.
3. Pour dry mix on a nonstick baking tray and spread it evenly.
4. Slide baking tray into the oven and leave to bake for 10 minutes while stirring every once in a while as it tends to get burnt if left unchecked.
5. Take it out of the oven and leave to cool.
6. Pour the cool mix into a bowl and add the chopped apples and walnuts, stirring constantly.
7. When it's completely mixed, serve with blueberry toppings and a cup of apple juice.

Spicy Shrimp Omelette

- Prep time: 5 minutes
- Cooking time: 20 minutes
- Serving: 2
- Classification: Main meal
- Age: 2 years and above

INGREDIENTS:

1. Chili garlic sauce
2. Eggs (2)
3. Olive oil (3 teaspoons)
4. Chopped shrimp, peeled (½ cup)
5. Water (4 tablespoons)
6. Sliced red bell pepper (½ cup)
7. Egg whites (4)
8. Salt
9. Black pepper powder

INSTRUCTIONS:

1. Warm the garlic sauce and 2 spoons of olive oil in a nonstick pan.
2. Pour in chopped shrimp and red peppers and sauté until it looks almost cooked.
3. Get a bowl, whisk the egg whites, whole eggs, black pepper, salt and water together.
4. Drizzle the last teaspoon of olive oil over the shrimp and pepper right before you add the egg mix.
5. Let it cook until the egg looks set. Flip once.
6. When both sides are set, serve with any garnish you like.

Low Glycemic Raspberry Muffins

- Prep time: 5 minutes
- Cooking time: 20 minutes
- Serving: 12
- Classification: Snack
- Age: 12 months and above

INGREDIENTS:

1. Soy flour (½ cup)
2. Brown sugar (⅓ cup)
3. Whole wheat flour (1 ½ cups)
4. Baking powder (2 teaspoons)
5. Soymilk (1 cup)
6. Cinnamon (2 teaspoons)
7. Raspberries (1 cup)
8. Egg whites (2)
9. Canola oil (2 tablespoons)

INSTRUCTIONS:

1. Prep oven by preheating to 190°F
2. Get a bowl large enough to mix all the dry ingredients and do just that.
3. Mix the wet ingredients in a different bowl.
4. Now pour the wet mix into the dry mix and mix for 2 minutes.
5. Add the raspberries.
6. Pour the batter into 12 muffin tins and bake for 20 minutes or until you stick it with a toothpick and it comes out dry.
7. Remove from the oven and leave to cool.
8. Serve!

Oat And Buckwheat Muesli With Pears And Grapes.

- Prep time: 5 minutes
- Cooking time: 10 minutes
- Serving: 6
- Classification: Main meal
- Age: 2 years and above

INSTRUCTIONS:

1. Puffed buckwheat (½ cup)
2. Cinnamon powder (2 teaspoons)
3. Rolled oats (1 ½ cups)
4. Diced fresh pears (1 cup)
5. Brown sugar (3 tablespoons)
6. Chopped dried apples (½ cup)
7. Halved red grapes (1 cup)
8. Rice milk

INSTRUCTIONS:

1. Prep oven by preheating to 325°F.
2. Get a nonstick baking tray and spread the rolled oats over it. Make this oat coating as even as possible.
3. Put it in the oven for 10 minutes while stirring every once in a while because they tend to get burnt pretty easily.
4. Take it out of the oven and set it aside to cool. Once cool enough, transfer it to a ceramic bowl with some water and leave it to soak overnight in the fridge.
5. Add chopped apples, cinnamon powder, puffed buckwheat and sugar to the now soaked oats and mix.
6. Serve with grape and pear toppings along with rice milk.

Chicken And Barley Soup

- Prep time: 5 minutes
- Cooking time: 1 hour
- Servings: 2
- Classification: Main meal
- Age: 2 years and above

INGREDIENTS:

1. Chicken broth (9 cups)
2. Chopped fresh celery (½ cup)
3. Chicken breast, skinned (1 ½ pound)
4. Diced fresh carrots (1 cup)
5. Cooked barley (½ cup)
6. Salt
7. Pepper
8. Cut fresh spinach leaves (½ cup)
9. Sliced yellow onion (¼ cup)

INSTRUCTIONS:

1. Dice the chicken into toddler bite sizes and put them in a pot with the chicken broth.
2. Aa soon as it boils, lower the heat and let it simmer for 45 minutes.
3. Throw in celery, onions and carrots. Leave to simmer for 17 minutes.
4. Throw in cooked barley, spinach, a pinch of salt and pepper.
5. When it is cooked through, set aside to cool.
6. Serve.

Hot Tomato Soup

- Prep time: 12 minutes
- Cooking time: 15 minutes
- Serving: 2
- Classification: Main meal
- Age: 2 years and above

INGREDIENTS:

1. Peeled and sliced shallots (3 oz)
2. Undrained stewed tomatoes (1 can)
3. Garlic (3 large cloves)
4. Olive oil (1 tablespoon)
5. Chili powder (½ teaspoon)
6. Salt (¼ teaspoon)
7. Chopped fresh basil leaves (2 tablespoons)
8. Apple cider vinegar (½ teaspoon)
9. Ground fresh red pepper)

INSTRUCTIONS:

1. Remove the skin of the garlic and crush it. Letting the crushed garlic sit for 6-9 minutes makes it more potent when it comes to health benefits.
2. While that is happening, pour the chicken broth, shallots, apple cider vinegar and tomatoes in a food processor and blitz until it is pasty smooth.
3. Pour olive oil into a nonstick pan that is set over medium heat. After 20 seconds, add the crushed garlic and chili powder. Leave it to cook for 35 seconds while stirring.
4. Now pour in the tomato mix and leave to boil.
5. Turn off the heat and sprinkle in the basil leaves.
6. For toddlers, let it cool for a bit before serving.

Sweet Spicy Red Pepper Hummus

- Prep time: 15 minutes
- Cooking time: 1 hour
- Serving: 2
- Classification: Side dish
- Age: 12 months and above

INGREDIENTS:

1. Roasted red peppers (1 jar)
2. Ground cumin (½ teaspoon)
3. Drained garbanzo beans (1 can)
4. Salt (¼ teaspoon)
5. Lemon juice (3 tablespoons)
6. Fresh parsley, chopped (1 tablespoon)
7. Minced tahini garlic (½ tablespoon)
8. Cayenne pepper (½ teaspoon)

INSTRUCTIONS:

1. Blitz the red peppers, fresh lemon juice, tahini, cumin, salt and cayenne pepper in a food processor until it looks almost smooth and a bit fluffy. Please use a spoon to take the mix off that's on the sides of the blender.
2. Pour it in a bowl and slide in the fridge. This should stay nothing less than 1 hour.
3. Don't serve cold and without parsley sprinkles.
4. Enjoy!

Chapter Seven: Recipes For Children Losing Teeth Or Are Lazy To Chew

Losing teeth is a very normal and somewhat exciting experience for kids. They start to get adult teeth, how cool is that? This turning point usually begins at 6 years old, so pay close attention to the little buggers because the Tooth Fairy will be here anytime now! Not like they won't tell you anyway...

Another thing you'll need to pay attention to is their diet. I'm no dentist, but I know for a fact that nobody can eat beef jerky right after they lose a tooth. Instead, they'll prefer softer, warmer foods that are still as healthy while their gums are still very sensitive. You wonder what to possibly feed them? Awesome recipes coming right up!

Strawberry Breakfast Bars

- Prep time: 35 minutes
- Cooking time: 40 minutes
- Serving: 8
- Classification: Snack
- Age: 2 years and above

INGREDIENTS:

Crust and topping:

1. Quick oats (1 cup)
2. Flour (½ cup)
3. Salt (¼ teaspoon)
4. Brown sugar (¼ cup)
5. Fresh orange (1 tablespoon)
6. Butter cubes (½ cup)

Bar filling:

1. Brown sugar (2 tablespoons)
2. Fresh orange juice (½ tablespoon)
3. Flour (1 tablespoon)
4. Sliced strawberries (11 oz)

INSTRUCTIONS:

1. Prep your oven by pre preheated to 375°F.
2. Now get a fairly sized pan and coat it with cooking spray or butter if that's what you have.
3. Put a mixture of sugar, flour and salt through a food processor and blitz a couple of times.
4. Dice the butter into bits and add it to the flour mix still in the food processor.
5. Blitz until everything is all mixed together.
6. Pour in the oats and blitz again.
7. Pour in half of the oat mix. That will be used to make the topping.
8. Now pour the orange juice into the other half of the oat mix and put it in a food processor and blitz until everything is mixed up.
9. Transfer the mix onto to prepped pan making sure to press it evenly into the pan.
10. For the filling, mix the flour, fresh orange juice and dark brown sugar in a bowl and throw in your strawberries. Mix again making sure all the strawberries get a bit of the flour mix.
11. Spread the filling evenly inside the pan with the oat crust.
12. Top with the other half of the oat mix we set aside earlier and coat with cooking spray.
13. Slide into the oven to bake for 45 minutes.

3 Minute Oatmeal

- Prep time: 1 minute
- Cooking time: 2 minutes
- Serving: 1
- Classification: Main meal
- Age: 12 months and above

INGREDIENTS:

1. Unsweetened almond milk (1 cup)
2. Cinnamon
3. Raisins/currants (4 tablespoons)
4. Rolled oats (½ cup)
5. Chia seeds (3 teaspoons)

INSTRUCTIONS:

1. Put the milk and rolled oats in a microwave-safe bowl and heat for about 2 minutes on high.
2. When the oats are ready, top with currants / raisins, cinnamon and chia seeds.
3. Let it cool before you serve.

Baked Mac & Cheese

- Prep time: 15 minutes
- Cooking time: 40 minutes
- Serving: 6
- Classification: Main meal
- Age: 2 years and above

INGREDIENTS:

1. Non-skimmed milk (2 cups)
2. Dry elbow macaroni shells (1 ½ cups)
3. Salt (½ teaspoon)
4. Butter (3 tablespoons)
5. Pepper (½ teaspoon)
6. All-purpose flour (3 tablespoons)
7. Shredded cheddar cheese (2 cups)

INSTRUCTIONS:

1. Prep oven by preheating to 350°F
2. Put salted water over medium high heat and let it boil. Now pour the pasta into the pot and cover it.

3. Now get a fairly large skillet, put it over medium heat and scoop the butter into it. Once it melts completely, pour in flour and stir constantly until mixture looks a bit brown. This should take 2 minutes or less.
4. Sprinkle some pepper and salt, stir. Pour in milk and whisk thoroughly to get rid of lumps that may form.
5. Leave the sauce to cook until it starts to thicken and bubble. This should take 5 to 7 minutes.
6. Now add the shredded cheese and stir or whisk until it's pasty smooth. Remove from heat.
7. At this point, the pasta should be almost cooked but still have a firm texture. Strain it, pour it into the sauce and toss to mix.
8. Transfer the pasta and sauce mix to a baking dish and bake until it starts to bubble and look brown. 25 minutes tops.
9. If you don't want to bake it to maintain the creaminess, just set it under a broiler until the top turns brown.
10. Serve!

Cheesy Zucchini Rice

- Prep time: 10 minutes
- Cooking time: 20 minutes
- Serving: 4 - 6
- Classification: Main meal
- Age: 2 years and above

INGREDIENTS:

1. Grated zucchini (1 medium size)
2. Long grain white rice (1 cup)
3. Sharp cheddar cheese, shredded (1 cup)
4. Low sodium chicken broth (2 cups)
5. Milk (2 tablespoons) This is optional.
6. Ground garlic (½ teaspoon)
7. Salt
8. Pepper

INSTRUCTIONS:

1. Mix the white rice and chicken broth in a pan which you'll put over the heat until it starts to boil.
2. It should be boiling now, lower the heat and leave it to simmer until most of the broth has been absorbed by the rice and it is soft. This should take 20 minutes.
3. Turn off the heat, add the zucchini, ground garlic and shredded cheese. Season it with pepper and salt or it won't have any flavour. Stir
4. This is where you can add milk if you want.
5. Serve and enjoy!

Twice Baked Cheese And Bacon Mashed Potato Casserole.

- Prep time: 15 minutes
- Cooking time: 40 minutes
- Serving: 8-10
- Classification: Main meal
- Age: 2 years and above

INGREDIENTS:

1. Butter (½ cup)
2. Cream cheese (6 oz)
3. Russet potatoes (3 lbs.)
4. Salt (½ teaspoon)
5. Parmesan cheese, grated (½ cup)
6. Crumbled cooked bacon (8 slices)
7. Heavy cream (½ cup)
8. Pepper (¼ teaspoon)
9. Shredded cheddar cheese (¾ cup)

INSTRUCTIONS:

1. Get a saucepan half-filled salted water and put potatoes on to boil. If the water isn't totally covering the potatoes, add a little more.
2. Once it boils, lower the heat and let it cook until it is soft. 15 minutes max. Now drain.
3. Mash the potatoes in a masher and add the cream cheese , heavy cream and butter. Mix thoroughly before sprinkling salt and pepper and mixing again.
4. Add the bacon strips, parmesan and cheddar cheese. Stir.
5. Prep your oven by heating to 350°F.
6. Pour the mashed potatoes into a casserole dish, top with any leftover cheese and bake for 25 minutes or more if it's not cooked through.
7. Let it cool before you serve it.

Homemade Baby Quinoa

- Prep time: 14 minutes
- Cooking time: 45 minutes
- Serving: 2
- Classification: Main meal
- Age: 6 - 12 months

INGREDIENTS:

1. Garlic powder (½ teaspoon)
2. Olive oil (1 tablespoon)
3. Diced zucchini (1 cup)
4. Diced onion (¼ medium size)
5. Dried thyme (½ teaspoon)
6. Diced eggplant (1 cup)
7. Diced green bell pepper (½ cup)
8. Fresh parsley (This is optional)
9. Quinoa (¼ cup)
10. Grated parmesan cheese (2 tablespoons). This is optional.
11. Chopped tomato (1)
12. Vegetable broth (1 cup)
13. Tomato paste (2 tablespoons)

INSTRUCTIONS:

1. Warm olive oil in a saucepan over medium low heat. Throw in the onions and sauté for 5 minutes. Add garlic powder, green pepper, dried thyme, tomato paste, chopped tomatoes, vegetable broth, eggplant, quinoa and zucchini. Leave it to simmer for about 20 minutes or more if the vegetables aren't soft and the quinoa hasn't sprouted. Feel free to add more broth at this point.
2. Turn off the heat and add the cheese and fresh parsley. Stir.
3. Pour the quinoa mix into a blender and pulse until smooth enough for your baby. Add water or vegetable broth for a thinner consistency.

Bacon-Parmesan Spaghetti Squash

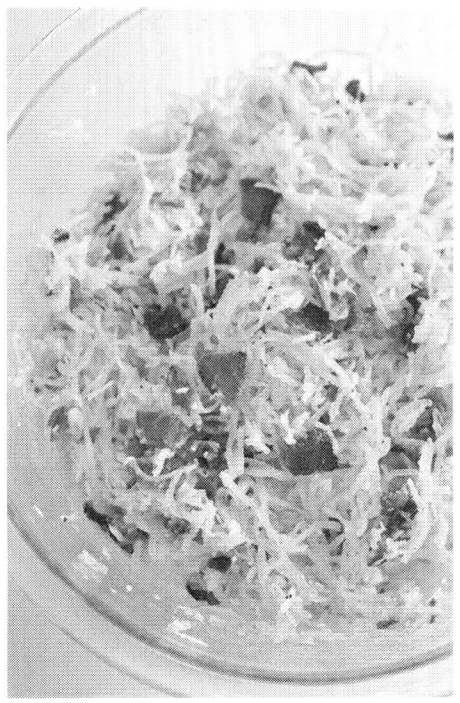

- Prep time: 10 minutes
- Cooking time: 1 hour
- Serving: 4
- Classification: Main meal
- Age: 2 years and above

INGREDIENT:

1. Shredded parmesan cheese (1 cup)
2. Bacon (1 pound)
3. Salt
4. Pepper
5. Spaghetti squash (1 large size)
6. Butter (¼ cup)

INSTRUCTIONS:

1. Prep oven by preheating to 375°F
2. Use parchment paper to coat a fairly big sized baking sheet.
3. Remove the stem end of the spaghetti squash and slice squash into rings. Use a spoon to get rid of the pulp and seeds from the rings.
4. Arrange squash rings on the lined baking sheet and bake for 45 minutes. The spaghetti strands should come off easily now if you scrape with a fork or something.
5. Meanwhile, you can't sit around for 45 minutes waiting for the squash rings to bake. Start chopping your bacon into bits. When it's ready, throw it into a pan and stir over medium heat until it is cooked through and very crispy. Remove from heat.
6. Time should be up for the squash rings so take them out of the oven and set aside to cool for a bit. Discard the shells of each squash ring and proceed to separate the strands. Using a fork, it's easier. Put the strands in a bowl when you're done.
7. Stir in butter and toss until all the butter melts. The heat from the squash strands should help do this if it's not warm enough, microwave it for 2 minutes.
8. Add crumbled bacon and parmesan cheese.
9. Sprinkle pepper and salt, stir then serve!

Garlic Parmesan Pasta

- Prep time: 10 minutes
- Cooking time: 20 minutes
- Serving: 4
- Classification: Main meal
- Age: 2 years and above

INGREDIENTS:

1. Chicken broth (2 cups)
2. Unsalted butter (2 tablespoons)
3. Grated parmesan cheese (¼ cup)
4. Raw fettuccine (8 oz)
5. Minced garlic (4 cloves)
6. Chopped parsley (2 tablespoons)
7. Milk
8. Kosher salt
9. Black pepper powder

INSTRUCTIONS:

1. Heat butter in a pan until it melts completely and stir in garlic. Leave it cook for 1 minute.
2. Pour in milk, raw fettuccine and chicken broth. Stir.
3. Sprinkle pepper and salt and leave it to boil.
4. Lower the heat as soon as it starts boiling and let it simmer for 20 minutes. Don't forget to stir every once in a while. The pasta should be thoroughly cooked if done right
5. Now add parmesan cheese and stir. If it's too thick, pour in milk until it's as thin as you'd like.
6. Top with chopped parsley and serve!

Slow Cooker Buttery Garlic Herb Mashed Potatoes

- Prep time: 10 minutes
- Cooking time: 4 hours
- Serving: 6
- Classification: Main meal
- Age: 12 months and above

INGREDIENTS:

1. Butter (4 tablespoons)
2. Dried parsley (2 teaspoons)
3. Chopped unpeeled red potatoes (2 pounds)
4. Plain Greek yogurt (½ cup)
5. Dried oregano (¼ teaspoon)
6. Minced garlic (1 tablespoon)

7. Milk (¼ cup)
8. Salt (2 teaspoons)
9. Dried basil (½ teaspoon)
10. Pepper (1 teaspoon)

INSTRUCTIONS:

1. Cook the chopped potatoes in a slow cooker on high for 3 hours. They should be soft and easy to pierce with a fork.
2. Throw in remaining ingredients leaving the butter to melt before you stir.
3. Mash the potatoes with a hand mixer.
4. Serve!

Heavenly Mashed Potatoes

- Prep time: 10 minutes
- Cooking time: 25 minutes
- Serving: 2
- Classification: Main meal
- Age: 12 months and above

INGREDIENTS:

1. Heavy cream (⅓ cup)
2. Minced garlic (2 cloves)
3. Peeled russet potatoes (4)
4. Cottage cheese puree (¼ cup)
5. Salt
6. Sliced chives (2 tablespoons)
7. Pepper
8. Unsalted butter (¼ cup)
9. Melted butter (For garnish)
10. Chives (For garnish)

INSTRUCTIONS:

1. Fill a fairly large pot with water and put the potatoes in to boil over medium heat.
2. The potatoes should be soft enough to pierce with a knife after 25 minutes so while we wait for that, get a small saucepan and stir in cream, garlic and butter. When it simmers, turn off the heat.
3. Back to the now soft potatoes. Drain the excess water and put the potatoes back in the pot to mash with a fork or wooden spatula. Sprinkle pepper and salt over the mash.
4. Drizzle cream over the mash slowly while stirring until you get a smooth paste.
5. Add the sliced chives and cottage cheese puree. Sprinkle on more seasoning if you like.
6. Serve with melted butter and chive toppings if you like.
7. Enjoy!

Cheesy Leftover Mashed Potato Pancakes

- Prep time: 20 minutes
- Cooking time: 5 minutes
- Serving: 12
- Classification: Main meal
- Age: 2 years and above

INGREDIENTS:

1. Lightly whisked egg (1)
2. Leftover mashed potatoes (2 cups)
3. Chopped green and white scallion parts (2 tablespoons)
4. All-purpose flour (3 tablespoons)
5. Shredded cheddar cheese (⅔ cup)
6. Vegetable oil
7. All-purpose flour (½ cup)
8. Sour cream

INSTRUCTIONS:

1. Mix the mashed potatoes, scallions, 3 tablespoons of all-purpose flour, cheese and eggs in a bowl.
2. Make 12 small portions out of this mix and roll each one into a compact ball right before you flatten it, creating a tiny pancake. Use your hands, it's much easier.
3. Pour the other portion of the all-purpose flour into a flat plate and dip each pancake in it to coat lightly.
4. Drizzle some vegetable oil onto a pan and fry the pancakes in sets. Make sure to flip every once in a while to ensure both sides are thoroughly cooked. Be sure to drizzle oil onto the pan before each set.
5. Set the pancakes on a plate lined with paper towels to drain the excess oil.
6. Sprinkle some salt over them and top with sour cream.
7. Bon Appetit!

Chapter Eight: Recipes For Children Who Hate Soups

Soups and kids are not exactly something you hear often mostly because kids absolutely hate greens. When they think greens, they think yuck which shouldn't be so surprising, even some adults hate greens. Soups are packed with nutrients that your kids are willing to forfeit because they just can't be bothered but as a parent, it's your job to be bothered. I'll tell you why:

- You get to sneak in the veggies and veggies are good, but some kids would rather run through every aisle in Walmart 8 times than eat a carrot. Soups are a brilliant way to get some extra vegetables into their diet without them even realising it!
- Some kids don't consume as much water as they should and guess what contains a lot of water? You got it! Soups.
- Ensuring your babies get the required amount of nutrients for proper development is important and seeing as soups are mostly veggies and meat, you definitely can't go wrong in that area.
- Let's accept it, a lot of cheap nutritious soups exist, so if you don't happen to have a lot of coins in your purse you can make a homemade delicacy for the little ones with next to nothing.
- Kids can get difficult to feed when they're healthy, imagine when they get sick and extremely cranky. Soups make it easy for them to get nutrients **and** water even when eating less than they normally would

I came up with a few kid-friendly soup recipes that might just turn them into Oliver Twist! Let's take a look :

Sweet potato and yellow split pea soup

- Prep time: 10 minutes
- Cooking time: 1 hour 11 minutes
- Serving: 2
- Classification: Main meal
- Age: 2 years and old

INGREDIENTS:

1. Chopped skinless sweet potato (1 small size)
2. Chopped onion (¼ cup)
3. Water (½ cup)
4. Ginger paste (½ teaspoon)
5. Toasted pumpkin seeds (½ teaspoon)
6. Dried yellow split peas (¼ cup)

INSTRUCTIONS:

1. Put some water in a pan and set it over medium heat, then throw in the onions and leave them to cook until they start to look translucent.
2. Pour in the ginger paste and stir fry.
3. Now add the yellow split peas, some more water and diced sweet potatoes. Leave it to boil before lowering the heat and leaving it to simmer for about 1 hour with the lid on.
4. Take off the lid and leave it to simmer for about 11 minutes.
5. Transfer the soup to a blender and blitz until you get a nice smooth puree.
6. Serve with pumpkin seed toppings.

Curried Pumpkin Soup

- Prep time: 10 minutes
- Cooking time: 35 minutes
- Serving: 1
- Classification: Main meal
- Age: 2 years and above

INGREDIENTS:

1. Cumin (½ teaspoon)
2. Diced onion (1 small size)
3. Coriander powder (½ tablespoon)
4. Olive oil (2 tablespoons)
5. Garlic paste (½ tablespoon)
6. Pumpkin puree
7. Coconut milk (½ cup)
8. Chicken stock (1 cup)
9. Curry powder (½ tablespoon)
10. Water (1 cup)
11. Salt

INSTRUCTIONS:

- Put a pan over medium heat and pour in the olive oil. After a minute, stir in onions and garlic paste and leave to cook until the onions are soft.
- Stir in the remaining spices and pumpkin puree.
- Pour in the chicken stock, milk and water. Stir and leave the soup to simmer for roughly 20 minutes.
- Turn off the heat and set the soup aside to cool.
- When it's cool enough, put it through a food processor and blitz until you get a smooth puree.
- Warm slightly before serving.

Taco Soup

- Prep time: 8 hours
- Cooking time: 12 hours
- Serving: 8
- Classification: Side dish
- Age: 2 years and above

INGREDIENTS:

1. Corn, frozen (1 bag)
2. Dried beans (1 pound)
3. Salt (1 teaspoon)
4. Taco seasoning mix
5. Rotel, frozen (1 can)
6. Ranch seasoning mix

INSTRUCTIONS:

1. Put beans in a bowl of water to soak for about 8 hours
2. Drain it to remove the excess water and rinse under running water.
3. Pour the beans in a crock pot filled with water and a packet of taco seasoning mix.

4. Put the crockpot over high heat and cook for 8 hours. The beans should be really soft then.
5. Sprinkle salt, ranch seasoning, Rotel and corn. Stir.
6. Lower the heat and leave it to simmer for 4 hours.
7. Garnish with a bit of shredded cheese, sour cream and tortilla chips.
8. Serve.

Pumpkin And Peanut Butter Soup

- Prep time: 10 minutes
- Cooking time: 20 minutes
- Serving: 4
- Classification: Main meal
- Age: 2 years and above

INGREDIENTS:

1. Garlic (2 cloves)
2. Olive oil (2 tablespoons)
3. Vegetable stock (1 liter)
4. One large onion
5. Soy sauce
6. Pumpkin squash
7. Peanut (½ cup)

INSTRUCTIONS:

1. Remove the skin and seeds of the pumpkin and cut it into tiny cubes.
2. Put olive oil in a pan and place over medium heat.
3. Cut the onions and throw it in the pan and stir fry until the whole room smells like onions, ha-ha. Shouldn't take long.
4. Pour in the garlic and stir for another 2 minutes.
5. Pour in the stock and pumpkin cubes and leave to simmer for about 20 minutes.
6. When it's all soft and ready, put it through a food processor and blend until a bit smooth.
7. Take out a cup of pumpkin soup and mix it in a separate bowl with soy sauce and peanut butter. Mix thoroughly.
8. Stir in the remaining soup and peanut butter soup mix into a pot. Add seasoning to adjust taste.
9. Serve and enjoy!

Beetroot Soup

- Prep time: 5 minutes
- Cooking time: 25 minutes
- Serving: 4
- Classification: Main meal
- Age: 2 years and above

INGREDIENTS:

Soup:

1. Carrots (2 medium size)
2. Olive oil (½ tablespoon)
3. Raw beetroot (500g)
4. White onion (1 small size)
5. Vegetable stock(1 liter)
6. Potatoes (200g)
7. Tomato puree (1 tablespoon)
8. Thyme (½ teaspoon)
9. Crushed garlic (2 cloves)
10. Pepper
11. Bay leaves (2)
12. Salt

Toppings:

1. Feta cheese (80g)
2. Creme fraiche (2 tablespoons)
3. Parsley (1 tablespoon)

INSTRUCTIONS:

1. Get the beetroot ready by trimming, peeling and chopping it into kid size chunks. Do the same for the carrots and potatoes.
2. Drizzle some oil onto a saucepan and warm it right before adding the onions and sautéing for 2 minutes.
3. Now add the crushed garlic and sauté for about a minute.
4. Stir in carrots, beetroot and potatoes and sauté for 3 minutes.
5. Now pour in tomato puree, thyme, stock and bay leaves. Stir and leave the mixture to boil before lowering the heat and leaving it to simmer for about 20 minutes.
6. Put the soup through a blender and blitz until smooth enough for your child.
7. Serve with parsley, creme fraiche and parsley toppings

Butternut and Peanut Butter Soup

- Prep time: 10 minutes
- Cooking time: 20 minutes
- Serving: 2
- Classification: Main meal
- Age: 12 months and above

INGREDIENTS:

1. Garlic (2 cloves)
2. Butternut squash (750g)
3. Olive oil (2 tablespoons)
4. Chicken stock (1 liter)
5. Onion (1 large size)
6. Soy sauce (1 teaspoon)
7. Peanut butter (½ cup)

INSTRUCTIONS:

1. Remove the skin and seeds of the butternut squash, then cut it into little cubes.
2. Pour olive oil in a pan and warm it over medium heat.
3. Cut the onion into little bits and stir for about a minute.
4. Throw in the garlic and stir fry for another 2 minutes.
5. Time to pour in the chicken stock and butternut squash
6. Leave it to dimmer for roughly 20 minutes. The butternut squash should be soft enough then. If not, add a few minutes.
7. Pour the soup in a blender and pulse.
8. Take out a cup of the smooth soup and mix it in a smaller bowl with soy sauce and peanut butter. Mix thoroughly.
9. Pour the peanut butter sauce and soup in a pot and stir.
10. This is the time to add any seasoning you like.
11. Serve and enjoy!

Italian Meatball and Gnocchi Soup

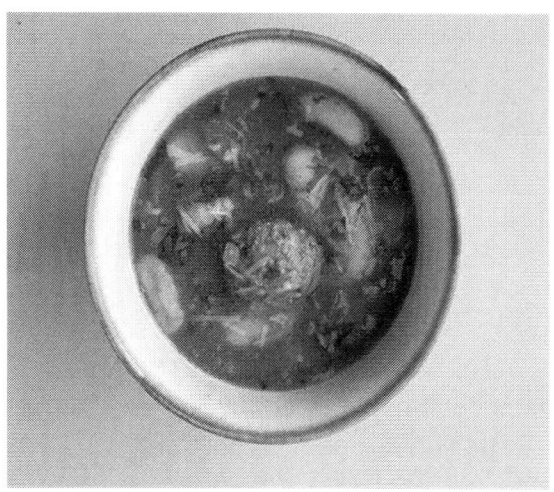

- Prep time: 5 minutes
- Cooking time: 5 hours
- Serving: 4
- Classification: Main meal
- Age: 2 years and above

INGREDIENTS:

1. Chopped onions (1 medium size)
2. Chopped celery (2 stalks)
3. Uncooked beef meatballs (12)
4. Chopped carrots (3 small size)
5. Chopped tomatoes (2 cans)
6. Tomato puree (2 tablespoons)
7. Crushed garlic (3 cloves)
8. Chicken stick (2 ½ cups)
9. Gnocchi (500g)
10. Dried oregano (1 teaspoon)

Garnishing:

1. Fresh basil leaves
2. Grated parmesan cheese

INSTRUCTIONS:

1. Put every ingredient but the parmesan, basil and gnocchi in a slow cooker and let it simmer for exactly 4 hours.
2. Now throw in the gnocchi and leave to simmer on low for another hour or 30 minutes if you're in a hurry, and put the heat on high.
3. Thin out the consistency if you want by adding some water or more chicken stock if you have any left.
4. Serve with basil and parmesan toppings.

Creamy Tomato Basil Soup with Grilled Cheese Bites

- Prep time: 10 minutes
- Cooking: 30 minutes
- Serving: 4
- Classification: Main meal
- Age : 2 years and above

INGREDIENTS:

1. Minced garlic (2 cloves)
2. Olive oil (2 tablespoons)
3. Kosher salt
4. Diced yellow onion (1 ¼ cup)
5. Whole peeled tomatoes + juice (1 can)
6. Chopped basil (½ cup)
7. Black pepper
8. Chopped fire-roasted tomatoes + juices (1 can)
9. Sugar (2 tablespoons)
10. Sourdough bread (8 slices pullman-style)
11. Balsamic vinegar (1 tablespoon)
12. Grated white cheddar cheese (2 cups)
13. Heavy cream (⅓ cup)

INSTRUCTIONS:

1. Get a large pot, drizzle exactly 1 tablespoon into it and let it warm over medium high heat for about 30 seconds. Throw in garlic and onions and leave to cook for 4 minutes. Sprinkle pepper and salt over garlic and onion mix.
2. Stir in both cans of tomatoes, juice and all while mashing the whole ones gently.
3. Now add a quarter cup of basil leaves, sugar and exactly 2 cups of water. Leave to boil.
4. Lower the heat and leave to simmer keeping the pot slightly open. 20 minutes max.
5. After 20 minutes, add the remaining basil, balsamic vinegar, pepper and salt.
6. Pour half of the soup into a blender, take out the hole at the top to let steam out and use a disposable dish towel to cover the hole if you don't want basil soup all in your face.
7. Now pulse a few times until it turns into a puree before transferring into a fresh pot. Do this to the remaining soup mixture.
8. Put soup pot over medium heat and add cream. Leave to simmer.
9. Turn off the heat and leave the pot covered.
10. Heat a nonstick grill pan coated with the remaining olive oil. Place about 4 slices of bread on a tray or clean worktable top. Spread ½ cup of cheese on each slice and top with the remaining 4 slices. Basically you should have a bread, cheese, bread arrangement.
11. Grill the sandwiches for 4 minutes, flipping once at 2 minutes. All the cheese should've melted by now and you should have a pretty brown crispy sandwich which you will now slice into 4 tiny squares.
12. Serve the soup with cream and basil toppings and a side of sandwiches.

Chapter Nine: Quick Kiddies Recipes

Easy Meatball Subs

- Prep time: 10 minutes
- Cooking time: 25 minutes
- Serving: 6
- Classification: Main meal
- Age: 2 years and above

INGREDIENTS:

1. Dried oregano (2 teaspoons)
2. Olive oil (1 ½ tablespoon)
3. Red pepper flakes (1 pinch)
4. Crushed garlic (2 cloves)
5. Sugar (½ teaspoon)
6. Crushed tomatoes (1 can)
7. Salt (1 ½ teaspoon)
8. Hot dog buns (6)
9. Rosina Italian style meatballs (1 pack)
10. Shredded mozzarella cheese (¾ cup)

INSTRUCTIONS:

1. Warm olive oil in a saucepan over medium heat for a few seconds.
2. Stir in oregano, red pepper flakes and garlic. Sauté for a minute before adding crushed tomatoes and stirring again.
3. Sprinkle salt and sugar while stirring constantly.
4. Time to add the meatballs. Toss them around in the sauce so they get completely coated. Now let it cook for 25 minutes properly covered. Stir every once in a while so it doesn't get burnt.
5. Raise the oven rack up a few bars and turn up the heat on the broiler.
6. Put the meatballs into the buns and sprinkle with cheese. Place them on the baking tray and leave to bake for 2 minutes.
7. When it's ready, set aside to cool.
8. Serve!

Quesadillas pizza bake

- Prep time: 5 minutes
- Cooking time: 6 minutes
- Serving: 1
- Classification: Main meal
- Age: 2 years and above

INGREDIENTS:

1. Shredded mozzarella cheese (¼ cup)
2. Pizza sauce (2 tablespoons)
3. Tortilla (1)

Optional ingredients:

1. Sliced pepperoni
2. Onions
3. Bell peppers
4. Grated parmesan cheese
5. Mushrooms
6. Sausage

Dipping:

1. Marinara sauce

INSTRUCTIONS:

1. Prep a large pan by preheating over medium heat.
2. Drizzle pizza sauce over a portion of the tortilla and spread.
3. Add the shredded cheese and any other of the additional ingredients you or your child likes. Cover toppings with more shredded mozzarella.
4. Fold tortilla on two.
5. Prep a griddle by coating with cooking spray. Place quesadillas in to cook until it's a bit brown. Cook each side for 2 minutes.
6. Turn off the heat and leave to cool before cutting into triangle shapes.
7. Serve.

Easy shepherd pie

- Prep time: 5 minutes
- Cooking time: 25 minutes
- Serving: 6
- Classification: Main meal
- Age: 2 years and above

INGREDIENTS:

1. Salt (1 teaspoon)
2. Ground beef (1 lb.)
3. Dried parsley (1 teaspoon)
4. Worcestershire sauce (½ tablespoon)
5. Pepper (1 teaspoon)
6. Minced garlic (1 teaspoon)
7. Flour (3 tablespoons)
8. Diced yellow onion (½ cup)

9. Butter (¼ cup)
10. Heavy cream (2 tablespoons)
11. Shredded cheddar cheese
12. Beef stock (1 ½ cup)
13. Frozen carrots and peas (12 oz)
14. McCajn smiles mashed potato shapes (½ pack)

INSTRUCTIONS:

1. Prep oven by preheating to 425°F.
2. Cook the mashed potato shapes according to the manufacturer's directions. Don't turn off the oven when you're done with the potato shapes.
3. While the potato shapes are cooking, get a frying pan and cook the beef, salt, parsley, pepper and Worcestershire sauce over medium heat until it is cooked through.
4. Strain excess oil and set aside in a bowl.
5. Sauté garlic and onions in the same pan over medium heat for about 3 minutes. Pour the onion and garlic mix into the bowl with the beef.
6. Melt butter on the same pan and stir in 3 tablespoons of flour until you form a pasty mixture.
7. Gradually stir in the beef stock. The resulting mix will be quite thick so don't look so surprised.
8. Throw in the ground beef mix, heavy cream and frozen veggies to the beef stock and stir fry for 5 minutes.
9. This is an opening for seasoning!
10. Scoop the beef mix into a muffin pan and sprinkle with shredded cheddar cheese and potato shapes.
11. Let this bake for 4 to 5 minutes. If the cheese isn't all melted by then, add a few extra minutes.
12. Serve warm.

Chicken Bacon Ranch Pull Apart Rolls

- Prep time: 10 minutes
- Cooking time: 40 minutes
- Serving: 12
- Classification: Snack
- Age: 2 years and above

INGREDIENTS:

1. Sliced deli chicken (1 lb.)
2. Colby jack cheese (12 slices)
3. 12-count potato rolls (1 package)
4. Butter (½ cup)
5. Garlic salt (1 teaspoon)
6. Crumbled cooked bacon (8 slices)
7. Onion powder (½ teaspoon)
8. Chopped fresh chives (1 tablespoon)
9. Shredded parmesan cheese (2 tablespoons)
10. Ranch salad dressing (⅓ cup)

INSTRUCTIONS:

1. Prep oven by preheating to 350 degrees.
2. Prep a fairly large baking sheet by lining with parchment paper.
3. Use a serrated blade to go through the center of the potato rolls. Arrange the bottoms of the rolls close to each other on the pan. Save the tops, you'll need them later.
4. Whip out a clean saucepan and place it over medium heat. Throw in the chives, softened butter, onion powder and garlic salt and stir gently until butter completely melts and everything is thoroughly mixed.
5. Use a brush to glaze the bottoms of the rolls with a third of the butter mixture.
6. Now you're going to put the Colby jack cheese right on top of the butter mixture on the potato rolls. Put the bacon crumbles and chicken right over that.
7. Pour some ranch dressing over the layers and add the last layer 9f Colby jack cheese. You're doing great!
8. Glaze again with the butter mixture and finally put the top of potato rolls over all those layers.
9. Glaze the top and sides of the potato rolls with the leftover butter mixture then top with shredded Parmesan cheese.
10. Lightly drape aluminum foil over it and leave to bake for about 20 minutes before discarding the foil and baking for an extra 10 minutes. If done right, the top should look a bit golden.
11. Serve with an extra drizzle of ranch dressing if you like.
12. Enjoy!

10 Minute Pizza Bake

- Prep time: 10 minutes
- Cooking: 25 minutes
- Serving: 8
- Classification: Snack
- Age: 2 years and above

INGREDIENTS:

1. Pizza sauce (1 jar)
2. Mozzarella cheese (2 cups)
3. Refrigerator biscuits (2
4. Pepperoni (30)
5. Insert desired pizza toppings here.

INSTRUCTIONS:

1. Prep oven by preheating to 350°F.
2. Coat a fairly large baking dish with nonstick cooking spray.
3. Use your hands to flatten the biscuits and place them on the pan. Spread some the pizza sauce over the biscuits and add the pepperoni and shredded cheese toppings.
4. Cover with another set of flat biscuits like a sandwich and top with the remaining cheese, pepperoni and pizza sauce.
5. Slide baking dish into the oven and leave to bake for roughly 25 minutes.
6. Cut the baked biscuits into little squares.
7. Serve!

Instant pot southern mac & cheese

- Prep time: 5 minutes
- Cooking time: 35 minutes
- Serving: 8
- Classification: Main meal
- Age: 2 years and above

INGREDIENTS:

1. Tillamook sharp cheddar cheese loaf (1 cup)
2. Hot sauce
3. Tillamook mozzarella shredded cheese (1 cup)
4. Tillamook special reserve extra sharp cheese loaf (1 cup)
5. Nutmeg (1 teaspoon)
6. Softened cream cheese (1 ounce)

7. Dry mustard powder (1 teaspoon)
8. Chicken stock (14 ½ oz)
9. Elbow macaroni noodles (1 lb.)
10. Water (2 cups)
11. Salt (½ teaspoon)
12. Tillamook unsalted sweet cream butter (1 ½ tablespoons)

INSTRUCTIONS:

1. Put water, chicken stock, mustard, butter, hot sauce, salt and nutmeg into a pot. Stir.
2. Now pour in the noodles and stir again. Thoroughly this time.
3. Put a lid on the pot, making sure it is sealed tight.
4. Cook for 6 minutes on high pressure.
5. Open the pot and throw in all the cheeses and mix well.
6. Serve warm.

Tex-Mex Chicken & White Cheddar Spaghetti

- Prep time: 10 minutes
- Cooking time: 20 minutes
- Serving: 4
- Classification: Main meal
- Age: 2 years and above

INGREDIENTS:

1. Butter (3 tablespoons)
2. All-purpose flour (2 tablespoons)
3. Grated white cheddar cheese(½ lb.)
4. Thin spaghetti (¾ lb.)
5. Milk (1 cup)
6. Diced yellow onion (1 cup)
7. Chicken stock (1 cup)
8. Chopped pickled Jalapeño + juice (1 tablespoon)
9. Cooked shredded chicken /2 cups
10. Cumin (½
11. Chopped cilantro (3 tablespoons)

INSTRUCTIONS:

1. Get a large pot, put some water in it. Just enough to cook the spaghetti. When the pasta is soft enough, drain all the water and set it aside in a bowl.
2. Lower the heat and throw butter into the pot to melt. Use the now melted butter to stir fry the onions for 5 minutes.
3. Add flour and leave to cook for 2 minutes.
4. Gently stir in milk and chicken broth. The slow stirring is to avoid lumps that may form.
5. Raise the heat to medium and stir in cheese until it melts completely.
6. Now add salt, jalapenos and juice, cumin, chicken, cilantro, pepper and cooked spaghetti. Stir until everything is well coated in the sauce.
7. Add more seasoning if you like.
8. Serve with cilantro toppings.

Chapter Ten: Kiddies Recipes High in Calcium and Iron

Iron and calcium are two very important nutrients when it comes to child development. Babies who are deficient in these nutrients are usually less active, are susceptible to slow growth, have pale skin, no appetite, the most unreasonable mood swings, anemia and others. Supplements can make up for the obvious lack, but diets play a huge role too. Foods like meat, fish, eggs, legumes, cereals, etc. should be a priority when planning meals. One doesn't need to be deficient to eat foods rich in calcium and iron. What's that thing they say? Prevention is better than cure, no?

Ready for some iron and calcium booster recipes?

Rustic Tomato Lentil Soup

- Prep time: 10 minutes
- Cooking time: 30 minutes
- Serving: 4
- Classification: Main meal
- Age: 2 years and above

INGREDIENTS:

1. Minced garlic
2. Olive oil (2 tablespoons)
3. Diced onion (1 medium size)
4. Chopped celery (2 stalks)
5. Diced carrots (3 medium size)
6. Vegetable stock (6 cups)
7. Cooked lentils (2 cups)
8. Dry pasta (1 cup)
9. Diced tomatoes and juice (1 can)
10. Cayenne
11. Pepper

INSTRUCTIONS:

1. Stir fry onions, carrots and garlic in a pot with some olive oil. Do this over medium high heat for 3 minutes or until the onions start to seem translucent.
2. Now you throw in the lentils, tomatoes and celery, sprinkle the peppers and pour in the vegetable stock. Let this boil before lowering the heat and leaving to simmer for about 20 minutes. The carrots should be soft enough to be run through by a fork now.
3. Pour in the pasta and leave to cook for 10 minutes or until soft enough.
4. Serve warm.

Baby beef casserole

- Prep time: 10 minutes
- Cooking time: 2 hours 35 minutes
- Serving: 8
- Classification: Main meal
- Age: 9 - 12 months

INGREDIENTS:

1. Flour (½ tablespoon l)
2. Sunflower oil (½ tablespoon)
3. Paprika (1 teaspoon)
4. Crushed garlic (1 clove)
5. Lean stewing steak (300g)
6. Chopped onion (1 small size)
7. Chicken stock (400ml)
8. Chopped potatoes (300g)
9. Parsley (1 sprig)
10. Sliced buttons mushrooms (110g)
11. Chopped carrots (200g)
12. Chopped celery (½ stick)
13. Thyme (This is optional)

INSTRUCTIONS:

1. Prep the oven by preheating to 300°F.
2. Drizzle oil into a casserole dish and stir fry the garlic and chopped onions for 3 minutes.
3. Get a small bowl, pour in the paprika and flour, mix well and use this to coat the meat, preferably by tossing it around in the bowl or some other method you find easy.
4. Fry the coated meat in the onion mix until both sides are brown.
5. Add the chicken stick and stir gently for a minute.
6. Stir in all the herbs and veggies and transfer the dish to the oven. Let it bake for 2 hours.
7. Should be 2 hours now, add mushrooms and leave to cook for extra 30 minutes.
8. Pour everything into a blender and pulse until smooth enough for your baby.
9. Serve warm.

Crockpot sweet potato lentils

- Prep time: 15 minutes
- Cooking time: 4 hours 30 minutes
- Serving: 6 - 8
- Classification: Main meal
- Age: 2 years and above

INGREDIENTS:

1. Minced onion (1 medium size)
2. Diced sweet potatoes (6 cups)
3. Salt (½ teaspoon)
4. Water (1 cup)
5. Vegetable broth (3 cups)
6. Ground coriander (2 teaspoons)

7. Coconut milk (1 can)
8. Garam masala (2 teaspoons)
9. Minced garlic (4 cloves)
10. Chili powder (2 teaspoons)
11. Raw red lentils (1 ½ cups)

INSTRUCTIONS:

1. Cook the vegetable broth, garlic, potatoes, spices and garlic in a crock pot over high heat for about 3 hours. The veggies should be soft now unless they're made of stone. Hopefully not.
2. Stir in the lentils, cover the pot and leave to cook for extra 1 ½ hours.
3. Now pour in coconut milk and enough water so it doesn't come out too thick.
4. Let it cool for a bit before you serve.

Apple, green beans and broccoli puree

- Prep time: 10 minutes
- Cooking time: 10 minutes
- Serving: 1
- Classification: Main meal
- Age: 6 months and above

INGREDIENTS:

1. Broccoli florets (½ cup)
2. Green beans (½ cup)
3. Fresh dessert apples (2 small size)

INSTRUCTIONS:

1. Slice the apple in half, remove the core and cut it into bits.
2. Trim the ends of the green beans then cut it into bits.
3. Prep a steamer over boiling water. Pour everything into the steamer and put the lid on.
4. Wait 10 minutes and check if the vegetables are soft enough to be run through by a fork. If yes, turn off the heat. If not, leave to cool for a few extra minutes.
5. Assuming everything is soft now, put it through a blender and pulse until it is smooth enough for your baby. Add some water to thin out the consistency if you want.
6. Leave to cool.
7. Serve!

Coconut rice pudding

- Prep time: 2 minutes
- Cooking time: 30 minutes
- Serving: 4
- Classification: Appetiser
- Age: 6 months and above

INGREDIENTS:

1. Coconut milk (100ml)
2. Pudding rice (½ cup)
3. Desiccated coconut (½ tablespoons)
4. Full fat milk (450ml)
5. Vanilla extract (½ teaspoon)

Toppings:

1. Chopped fruit of choice
2. Fruit compote
3. Sugar free jam

INSTRUCTIONS:

1. Put every ingredient in a saucepan that has a heavy bottom, sort of. Wait till it boils then lower the heat and leave to simmer for 30 minutes with the lid on
2. All the milk should have been absorbed by the rice now, so turn off the heat.
3. Serve warm with any topping of your choice.

Baby beef puree

- Prep time: 5 minutes
- Cooking time: 25 minutes
- Serving: 1 ½
- Classification: Main meal
- Age: 4 months and above

INGREDIENTS:

1. Dried oregano (1 teaspoon)
2. Cubes sirloin (8 oz)
3. Beef broth (2 cups)

INSTRUCTIONS:

1. Cook broth, dried oregano and beef in a medium pot set over medium heat. Let it boil before lowering the heat and leaving to simmer for about 25 minutes or more if the beef isn't cooked through at 25 minutes.
2. Leave it to cool before putting only the beef through a food processor. Pulse while adding a little broth in between pulses until the consistency is right for your baby.
3. Serve!

Dried beans puree

- Prep time: 3 minutes
- Cooking time: 3 hours max.
- Serving: 2
- Classification: Main meal
- Age: 8-12 months

INGREDIENTS:

1. Dried beans (1 cup)

INSTRUCTIONS:

1. Put the beans in a pot filled with water and leave to soak overnight.
2. The next day, change the water and place the pot over high heat to boil.
3. Lower the heat and leave to simmer for **1 hour** if you're using large lima beans, **50 minutes** if you're using baby lima beans, **1 hour 15 minutes** if you're using garbanzo beans, small white beans, pinto beans, red kidney beans, great northern beans and black beans and **3 hours** if you're using soybeans.
4. Strain all the water from the beans and blitz in a blender. Use breast milk or water to thin out the consistency.
5. Serve warm.

Chapter Eleven: Kiddies Recipes High in Vitamins

Broccoli potato and cheese puree

- Prep time: 1 minute
- Cooking time: 10 minutes
- Serving: 6
- Classification: Main meal
- Age: 8-12 months

INGREDIENTS:

1. White cheddar cheese (2 tablespoons)
2. Diced potato (1 large size)
3. Chopped broccoli (1 cup)

INSTRUCTIONS:

1. Cook the potatoes for 6 minutes in a steamer pot filled with boiling water.
2. Pour in broccoli and cook for another 4 minutes or until a fork is easily able to go through the veggies.
3. Pour everything in a blender and pulse until smooth.
4. Serve cool.

Kiddies granola bar

- Prep time: 15 minutes
- Cooking time: 35 minutes
- Serving: 4
- Classification: Snack
- Age: 2 years and above

INGREDIENTS:

1. Wheat germ (½ cup)
2. Rolled oats (2 cups)
3. Brown sugar (¾ cup)
4. All-purpose flour (1 cup)
5. Salt (¾ teaspoon)
6. Cinnamon powder (¾ teaspoon)
7. Raisins (¾ cup) This is optional
8. Vegetable oil (½ cup)
9. Honey (½ cup)
10. Vanilla extract (2 teaspoons)
11. Whisked egg (1 small size)

INSTRUCTIONS:

1. Prep oven by preheating to 350°F.
2. Coat a baking pan with nonstick cooking spray or butter.
3. Mix the wheat germ, oats, cinnamon raisins, brown sugar, salt and flour in a bowl making a nice round well in the middle.
4. Now you're going to fill your well with the egg, vanilla extract, honey and vegetable oil.
5. Use your hands to mix everything thoroughly before transferring the mix to the greased pan.
6. Let this bake until the bars start to brown. It usually takes 35 minutes tops.
7. Set aside to cool for just 5 minutes before cutting into little squares or whatever shape you like.
8. Serve!

Skewered grilled potatoes

- Prep time: 20 minutes
- Cooking time: 1 hour 20 minutes
- Serving: 2
- Classification: Main meal
- Age: 2 years and above

INGREDIENTS:

1. Water (½ cup)
2. Dry white wine (¼ cup)
3. Diced red potato (2 pounds)
4. Wooden skewers (prep by soaking in water for 30 minutes)
5. Light mayonnaise (½ cup)
6. Garlic powder (1 teaspoon)
7. Dried rosemary, crushed (2 teaspoons)

INSTRUCTIONS:

1. Cook potatoes inside a bowl of water in a microwave set on high heat for 15 minutes.
2. Remove the water and set the potatoes aside to dry for a bit.
3. Mix rosemary, mayonnaise, garlic powder and white wine in a bowl large enough to fit the potatoes.
4. Now stir in the potatoes, making sure to coat every inch in the sauce.
5. Place it in the fridge to marinate for an hour.
6. Grease an outdoor grill and set the heat to high.
7. The potatoes should be done marinating. Now skewer and grill for 8 minutes occasionally glazing with marinade and flipping every now and then so all the sides get cooked through.
8. Remove the skewers and serve cool.

Broccoli marinara

- Prep time: 5 minutes
- Cooking time: 20 minutes
- Serving: 2
- Classification: Main meal
- Age: 2 years and above

INGREDIENTS:

1. Chopped garlic(1 clove)
2. Olive oil (1 tablespoon)
3. Broccoli florets (½ pound)
4. Salt
5. Diced tomatoes + olive oil, balsamic vinegar and basil (½ can)
6. Pepper

INSTRUCTIONS:

1. Warm the oil in a pan set over medium heat.
2. Stir fry garlic in oil for a few minutes before adding tomatoes and leaving to simmer until the liquid reduces by half.
3. Throw in the broccoli florets and sprinkle the pepper and salt. Leave everything to simmer for about 10 minutes over low heat with the lid on.
4. Try not to overcook the broccoli because that will make it appear somewhat dull.
5. Stir before serving.

Golden oatmeal

- Prep time: 5 minutes
- Cooking time: 7 minutes
- Serving: 1
- Classification: Main meal
- Age: 12 months and above

INGREDIENTS:

1. Sliced banana (½ finger)
2. Water (1 cup)
3. Turmeric powder (¼ teaspoon)
4. Rolled oats (½ cup)
5. Peanut butter (1 tablespoon)
6. Cinnamon powder (½ teaspoon)

INSTRUCTIONS:

1. Cook oats in a saucepan with some water.
2. If it's clearly boiling, lower the heat and sprinkle in turmeric and banana.
3. Leave mixture to simmer for 5 minutes until the consistency seems right for your baby.
4. Turn off the heat and add cinnamon powder. Stir for a few minutes and cover the pan to let the oatmeal thicken. 2 minutes tops.
5. Serve with peanut butter topping.

Blackberry pie oatmeal

- Prep time: 5 minutes
- Cooking time: 10 minutes
- Serving: 1
- Classification: Main meal
- Age: 12 months and above

INGREDIENTS:

1. Egg (1 small size)
2. Water (1 cup)
3. Blackberry flavored yogurt (6 oz)
4. Rolled oats (½ cup)
5. Unsweetened applesauce (⅓ cup)
6. Salt

INSTRUCTIONS:

1. Stir oats into a saucepan with salted water and leave to boil.
2. Stir in egg until everything is all mixed up.
3. Lower the heat and leave oats to simmer for 5 minutes or until the egg is cooked through.
4. Add applesauce and yogurt. Mix well.
5. Serve.

Pumpkin spinach toddler muffins

- Prep time: 15 minutes
- Cooking time: 1 hour 5 minutes
- Serving: 2
- Classification: Snack
- Age: 2 years and above

INGREDIENTS:

1. Eggs (3 small size)
2. Maple syrup (¼ cup)
3. Rolled oats (1 cup)
4. Canned pumpkin (2 cups)
5. Olive oil (½ cup)
6. Whole wheat flour (1 cup)
7. Nutmeg powder (½ teaspoon)
8. Baking soda (1 teaspoon)
9. Spinach (½ cup)
10. Baking powder (1 teaspoon)
11. Cinnamon powder (½ teaspoon)

INSTRUCTIONS:

1. Prep oven by preheating to 350°F.
2. Coat two muffin tins with nonstick cooking spray or paper liners.
3. Mix eggs, maple syrup, pumpkin and olive oil in a large bowl.
4. Mix all the dry ingredients in a smaller bowl and stir it into the large bowl.
5. Stir in spinach and scoop mixture into greased muffin tins.
6. Bake for 20 minutes or until cooked through.
7. Leave to cool before taking the cake out of the tins.
8. Serve.

Chapter Twelve: Kiddies Salad Recipes

Salads in general are totally healthy and delicious, but for kids are totally different from salads for adults because their palates are still tender and developing. Point is, when preparing kid's salads, the best path to tread is the simple path. You can never go wrong with simple but tasty and familiar ingredients.

Some kids are usually not open to the idea of a salad so take it slow, ease them into it and when they start having salad cravings or wolfing down plates of salad, you can always add them to the preparations. It keeps them busy and interested in trying new kinds of salads. Plus it's totally fun. I cooked up a few delish salad recipes that I bet your kids will drool over in no time. You can always modify the ingredients to your child's tastes but remember, keep it as simple as you can.

Rainbow veggie rice noodle salad

- Prep time: 5 minutes
- Cooking time: 5 minutes
- Serving: 4
- Classification: Main meal
- Age: 2 years and above

INGREDIENTS:

Salad:

1. Red pepper (1 medium size)
2. Sweet corn (2 tablespoons)
3. Carrot (1 large size)
4. Sesame seeds (1 tablespoon)
5. Zucchini (1 medium size)
6. Red cabbage (1 small size)
7. Dry rice noodles (90g)
8. Tender stem broccoli (8 stalks)

Dressing:

1. Fresh lime juice(½ small size)
2. Sesame oil (1 tablespoon)
3. Cold water (½ tablespoon)
4. Sweet chili sauce (1 tablespoon)

INSTRUCTIONS:

1. Put a kettle filled with water over medium heat and wait for it to boil.
2. You don't have to sit around waiting for it to boil, get busy on your salad. Grate your carrot and zucchini into a bowl. Slice the pepper and red cabbage into the same bowl.
3. Throw in sesame seeds and sweet corn.
4. Dice the broccoli into tiny bits and put in a saucepan filled with boiling water from the kettle.
5. Let this cook for 3 minutes over high heat before turning off the heat, pour in the rice noodles and leave covered for about 5 minutes.
6. Meanwhile, mix all the dressing ingredients in a cup, adding a little water when necessary to thin out the consistency.
7. The rice noodles should be soft now so go ahead to drain the water and transfer the noodles and broccoli to the salad bowl. Stir in the dressing and serve in tiny bowls.

Child friendly hummus with crudités

- Prep time: 2 minutes
- Cooking time: 0 minutes
- Serving: 2
- Classification: Dessert.
- Age: 2 years and above

INGREDIENTS:

1. Fresh lemon juice (1 tablespoon)
2. Cooked chickpeas + juice (1 can)
3. Crushed garlic (1 clove)
4. Olive oil (3 tablespoons)
5. Tahini (1 teaspoon)

INSTRUCTIONS:

1. Throw every ingredient except olive oil in the food processor and blitz until completely smooth. Add a little olive oil in between pulses until everything is properly mixed together.
2. To thin out the consistency of the hummus, use the juice from a ghee chickpea can.
3. Serve in bowls with crudités like cucumber, pepper, carrot, sugar snap peas and celery.

Rainbow chicken salad

- Prep time: 10 minutes
- Cooking time: 15 minutes
- Serving: 2
- Classification: Main meal
- Age: 2 years and above

INGREDIENTS:

Salad:

1. Cabbage (1 cup)
2. Red bell pepper (1 medium size)
3. Chicken breast (1 pound)
4. Carrot (1 medium size)
5. Chopped red cabbage (2 cup)
6. Orange bell pepper (1 medium size)
7. Green onion (2 stalks)
8. Avocado (1 medium size)
9. Peanuts (¼ cup)
10. Cilantro (1 cup)

Dressing:

1. Water (2 tablespoons)
2. Low sodium soy sauce (2 tablespoons)
3. Organic peanut butter (½ cup)
4. Honey (2 tablespoons)
5. Rice wine vinegar (2 tablespoons)
6. Sesame oil (¼ teaspoon)
7. Lime (1 medium size)

INSTRUCTIONS:

1. Place the chicken in a saucepan with water until cooked through. Now cut it into bits, it should fill 3 cups.
2. Cut the peppers, cilantro, avocado, onions and Peanuts into a large bowl. Grate and shred the carrot and cabbage respectively.
3. In a different bowl, mix all the dressing ingredients adding a little hot water to thin out the consistency.
4. Pour the dressing into the salad bowl and mix thoroughly.
5. Serve!

Carrot, Courgetti & Avocado Salad

- Prep time: 10 minutes
- Cooking time: 0 minutes
- Serving: 6
- Classification: Side dish
- Age: 2 years and above

INGREDIENTS:

Salad:

1. Sesame seeds (2 tablespoons)
2. Zucchini (1 medium size)
3. Chopped avocado (1 medium size)
4. Chopped red pepper (1 medium size)
5. Peeled carrot (1 large size)
6. Salad leaves (100g)

Dressing:

1. Honey (1 tablespoon)
2. Olive oil (2 tablespoons)
3. Fresh lime juice (½ tablespoon)
4. Vinegar (1 tablespoon)
5. Soy sauce (½ tablespoon)

INSTRUCTIONS:

1. Put the salad leaves in a bowl and set aside.
2. Wash the other veggies under clean running water.
3. Grate the zucchini, put it in between some kitchen paper and squeeze to get rid of a lot of moisture. Once that's done, put it in a bowl.
4. Grate the carrots over the zucchinis and throw in the red pepper, avocado and sesame seeds. Mix mix mix.
5. Pour all the dressing ingredients in a jar, cover it and shake as hard as you can to mix.
6. Drizzle over the zucchini mix.
7. Bring the bowl of salad leaves and gently transfer the zucchini mix to it.
8. Serve.

Papaya noodle salad

- Prep time: 15 minutes
- Cooking time: 0 minutes
- Serving: 6
- Classification: Side dish
- Age: 2 years and above

INGREDIENTS:

1. Sliced red capsicum (½)
2. Chopped Lebanese cucumber(1)
3. Cubed papaya(500g)
4. Rice vermicelli (½ pack)
5. Chopped cherry tomatoes (250g)
6. Quartered lime (1)
7. Vietnamese salad dressing
8. Rocket and spinach mix leaves (160g)

INSTRUCTIONS:

1. Cook the rice vermicelli in a pot of boiling water for 2 minutes. Drain and rinse under cold running water.
2. Mix the veggies and noodles in a bowl and drizzle Vietnamese dressing all over it.
3. Squeeze a bit of lime over it and serve immediately.

Avocado & strawberry macaroni pasta salad

- Prep time: 3 minutes
- Cooking time: 8 minutes
- Serving: 4
- Classification: Main meal
- Age: 2 years and above

INGREDIENTS:

Salad:

1. Strawberries (10-15)
2. Avocado (1 medium size)
3. Sweetcorn (4 tablespoons)
4. Macaroni (2 cups)
5. Green pepper (1 medium size)

Dressing:

1. Fresh lime juice (1 medium size)
2. Olive oil (2 tablespoons)

INSTRUCTIONS:

1. Put water in a pot to boil.
2. Pour in the pasta and leave to cook for 10 minutes.
3. Now drain the water and leave pasta in the sieve for it to cool.
4. Chop the strawberries, pepper and avocado into a bowl.
5. Pour in the now cool pasta and toss.
6. This is the time to add any seasoning of choice.
7. Pour the dressing ingredients into a jar and shake to mix.
8. Drizzle dressing over pasta salad and serve.

Potato salad for babies

- Prep time: 5 minutes
- Cooking time: 10 minutes
- Serving: 1
- Classification: Main meal
- Age: 9 months

INGREDIENTS:

1. Powdered pepper (⅛ teaspoon)
2. Chopped coriander leaves (1 teaspoon)
3. Powdered cumin (⅛ teaspoon)
4. Salt
5. Potato (2 small size)
6. Fresh lemon juice (1 teaspoon)

INSTRUCTIONS:

1. Prep the baby's feeding utensils by soaking in hot water for 5 minutes.
2. Wash the potatoes and put them in a pressure cooker filled with water. Leave it to cook over medium heat for 10 minutes.
3. Remove the potatoes and set them aside to cool enough for you to hold them.
4. Remove the skin and dice them into bits.
5. Mix cumin, lemon juice, pepper and salt in a large bowl.
6. Throw in potatoes cubes and stir gently so you don't mash them unintentionally.
7. Serve with coriander leaf toppings.

Chapter Thirteen: Kiddies Cookie Recipes.

Cookies are usually the go-to when it comes to appeasing a fussy child or even adults. We all love cookies. The little ones can't be torn away from their treats, so inexpensive homemade and absolutely delicious treats are starting to seem like a great idea, right?

On the plus side, the kids can help out, that is if they don't eat all the ingredients first. Sounds like a fun playdate to me!

Chocolate Chip Pudding Cookies

- Prep time: 10 minutes
- Cooking time: 10 minutes
- Serving: 48
- Classification: Snack
- Age: 2 years and above

INGREDIENTS:

1. Brown sugar (¾ cup)
2. Butter (2 sticks)
3. Vanilla (½ teaspoon)
4. White sugar (¾ cup)
5. Any instant pudding flavour (1 oz)
6. Salt (1 teaspoon)
7. Eggs (2)
8. Chocolate chips (12 oz)
9. Baking soda (1 teaspoon)

10. All-purpose flour (2 ½ cups)

INSTRUCTIONS:

1. Whisk the butter and sugars in a bowl.
2. Add instant pudding powder, vanilla and eggs. Whisk.
3. Get a different bowl and in it, you'll mix the flour, salt and baking soda.
4. Now pour the dry ingredients into the wet ingredients and mix with your hands. Keep adding flour until the batter stops getting stick to the walls of the bowl.
5. Throw in chocolate chips and fold gently ensuring there's a chocolate chip per square inch
6. Make little balls from the batter and arrange them on a baking pan.
7. Leave it to bake for about 10 minutes. The cookies should look golden if done right.
8. Remove from the oven and leave to cool.
9. Serve.

Cream Cheese Cookie Recipe

- Prep time: 15 minutes
- Cooking time: 15 minutes
- Serving: 36
- Classification: Snack
- Age: 2 years and above

INGREDIENTS:

1. White sugar (1 cup)
2. Softened butter (¾ cup)
3. Egg yolks (3)
4. Cream cheese (¼ cup)
5. Brown sugar (¼ cup)
6. Flour (2 ½ cups)
7. Cream of tartar (½ teaspoon)
8. Vanilla (1 teaspoon)
9. Baking soda (1 teaspoon)

INSTRUCTIONS:

1. Prep the oven by preheating to 350°F.
2. Use a hand mixer to whisk the butter, sugars and cheese.
3. Add vanilla and egg yolks. Whisk!
4. Turn off the hand mixer and get a spatula. Stir in baking soda, cream of tartar and the flour.
5. Scoop a bit of the cookie dough and place it on a non-greased baking sheet with enough space in between each cookie.
6. Leave to bake for about 15 minutes.
7. Set aside to cool.
8. Serve.

Apple Cookies

- Prep time: 20 minutes
- Cooking time: 15 minutes
- Serving: 36
- Classification: Snack
- Age: 2 years and above

INGREDIENTS:

1. White sugar (¾ cup)
2. Eggs (2)
3. Softened butter (½ cup)
4. Vanilla (1 teaspoon)
5. Brown sugar (½ cup)
6. Baking powder (1 teaspoon)
7. Cinnamon (2 teaspoons)
8. Flour (1 cup)
9. Salt (½ teaspoon)
10. Chopped almonds (1 cup)
11. Nutmeg (1 teaspoon)
12. Rolled oats (1 cup)
13. Chopped apples (1½ cups)

INSTRUCTIONS:

1. Prep oven by preheating to 350°F. Think of it as cookie temperature.
2. Now mix the butter and sugars thoroughly until you get a creamy result.
3. Whisk in eggs and vanilla.
4. Get a different bowl for the dry ingredients, pour and mix all of them.
5. Add the dry ingredients to the wet ingredients and mix thoroughly.
6. Throw in almonds, oats and apples.
7. Scoop cookie dough and place them on a baking sheet lined with parchment paper.
8. Let it bake for about 15 minutes.
9. Leave to cool before serving.

Classic Chocolate Chip Cookies

- Prep time: 5 minutes
- Cooking time: 10 minutes
- Serving: 4
- Classification: Snack
- Age: 2 years and above

INGREDIENTS:

1. White sugar (1 cup)
2. Vanilla extract (2 teaspoons)
3. Softened butter (1 cup)
4. Brown sugar (1 cup)
5. Salt (½ teaspoon)
6. Eggs(2)
7. Hot water (2 teaspoons)
8. All-purpose flour (3 cups)
9. Baking soda (1 teaspoon)
10. Semi-sweet chocolate chips (2 cups)

INSTRUCTIONS:

1. Prep oven by preheating to our cookie temperature, 350°F.
2. Mix the sugars and butter with a hand mixer until it gets creamy and smooth.
3. Whisk in the eggs first then the vanilla extract.
4. Mix the baking soda and hot water in a different bowl before adding it to the batter.
5. Sprinkle salt.
6. Stir in flour and chocolate chips using a spatula.
7. Scoop the dough and place fairly sized spoonfuls on a baking sheet lined with parchment paper.
8. Leave to bake for 10 minutes
9. Serve cool.

Pumpkin Spice Cranberry Cookie

- Prep time: 10 minutes
- Cooking time: 12 minutes
- Serving: 12
- Classification: Snack
- Age: 2 years and above

INGREDIENTS:

1. Pumpkin pie spice (½ teaspoon)
2. Oats (1 cup)
3. Honey (1 ½ teaspoons)
4. Pumpkin puree (½ can)
5. Dried cranberries (¼ cup)
6. Vanilla (½ teaspoon)

INSTRUCTIONS:

1. Prep oven to cookie temp.
2. Pour everything except the cranberries in a bowl and mix thoroughly.
3. Once you get everything all mixed up, add the cranberries and mix again, gently this time.
4. Scoop the dough onto a greased baking sheet and use your hands to flatten them because they can't do that on their own. Greasing the pan is very important seeing as the dough doesn't contain any butter
5. Let this bake for 12 minutes or until the cookies have hardened.
6. Serve cool.

Shortbread Cookies

- Prep time: 10 minutes
- Cooking time: 10 minutes
- Serving: 36
- Classification: Snack
- Age: 2 years and above

INGREDIENTS:

1. Vanilla extract (2 teaspoons)
2. Sugar (¾ cup)
3. Flour (2 cups)
4. Butter (¾ cup)
5. Salt (⅛ teaspoon)

INSTRUCTIONS:

1. Use a hand mixer to cream the sugar and butter in a bowl.
2. Sprinkle the salt and pour in the vanilla. Mix thoroughly.
3. Stir in flour with a spatula then mix thoroughly with your hand mixer.
4. If you happen to not own a mixer, you can knead the flour with your hands. The kids can totally help out with this step.
5. Sprinkle flour on a clean flat surface and use a rolling pin to spread the dough out as evenly as you can. Not too thin, however.
6. Now carve out any shapes you want.
7. Arrange the cookie shapes on a greased baking sheet and leave to bake for 10 minutes.
8. When they're ready, leave them to cool on the sheet for about a minute before transferring them to a rack.
9. Decorate with icing or serve without.

Carrot Cake Cookie

- Prep time: 10 minutes
- Cooking time: 15 minutes
- Serving: 40
- Classification: Snack
- Age: 2 years and above

INGREDIENTS:

1. Eggs (2)
2. Brown sugar (½ cup)
3. Grated carrots (1 cup)
4. Butter (½ cup)
5. Dried cranberries (1 cup)
6. Salt (½ teaspoon)
7. White sugar (½ cup)
8. Flour (2 cups)
9. Allspice (½ teaspoon)
10. Baking soda (½ teaspoon)
11. Nutmeg powder (½ teaspoon)
12. Baking powder (1 teaspoon)
13. Cinnamon powder (1 tablespoon)
14. Chopped pecans (½ cup)

INSTRUCTIONS:

1. Prep oven to cookie temperature.
2. I bet you can guess what happens at this point. Whip out your hand mixer and cream the sugars and butter guys!
3. Add the carrots, dried cranberries and eggs. Whisk!
4. Mix all the dry ingredients in a different bowl.
5. Now pour the dry ingredients into the wet ingredients and use your hands to mix properly.
6. Now add the pecans and fold them in.
7. Scoop the dough and place on a greased baking sheet.
8. Leave to bake for about 15 minutes.
9. Transfer to rack to cool.
10. Serve.

No-Bake Cookies

- Prep time: 40 minutes
- Cooking time: 10 minutes
- Serving: 24 cookies
- Classification: Snack
- Age: 2 years and above.

INGREDIENTS:

1. Unsalted butter (½ cup)
2. Oats (3 cups)
3. Sugar (2 cups)
4. Creamy peanut butter (1 cup)
5. Milk (½ cup)
6. Vanilla extract (1 tablespoon)
7. Cocoa powder (¼ cup)

INSTRUCTIONS:

1. Boil the milk, cocoa powder, sugar and butter in a fairly sized pot. Stir constantly.
2. Turn off the heat and stir in oats, peanut butter and vanilla.
3. Scoop the cookie dough and place on a parchment-lined flat surface. Leave it to set for 30 minutes.

Chewy-Crispy Peanut Butter Cookies

- Prep time : 12 minutes
- Cooking time: 13 minutes
- Serving: 10
- Classification: Snack
- Age: 2 years and above

INGREDIENTS:

1. Granulated sugar (¾ cup)
2. Unsalted butter) ¾ cup)
3. Honey (1 tablespoon)
4. Creamy peanut butter (½ cup)
5. Light brown sugar (½ cup)
6. All-purpose flour (2 cups)
7. Salt (¼ teaspoon)
8. Vanilla extract (1 ½ teaspoons)
9. Baking soda (1 teaspoon)
10. Eggs (2)

INSTRUCTIONS:

1. Prep oven by preheating to 350°F
2. Prep two baking sheets with parchment paper and go on to do other things like mixing the peanut butter, ½ granulated sugar, unsalted butter, honey and brown sugar in a bowl..
3. Get a fresh bowl and cream your sugar and butter until it's really fluffy and pale, sort of.
4. Stir in vanilla extract and egg whisking for about 1 minute.
5. Reduce the mixer's speed, all the dry ingredients and mix properly.
6. Make a cookie ball with your hands, dip the ball in the bowl of granulated sugar .and place on the sheet. Now gently palm the cookie ball to flatten it. Repeat process until there's no cookie dough left.
7. Let them bake for 13 minutes. If done right, they should have cracks on the top and brown edges.
8. Leave the cookies on the sheets for 5 minutes to cool before transferring them to a wire rack.
9. Serve.

Banana Oatmeal Cookies

- Prep time: 10 minutes
- Cooking time: 15 minutes
- Serving: 12
- Classification: Snack
- Age: 2 years and above

INGREDIENTS:

1. 1-minute oatmeal (¾ cup)
2. Ripe bananas (2 fingers)
3. Chocolate chips (⅓ cup
4. Crunchy peanut butter (¼ cup)

INSTRUCTIONS:

1. Prep oven 350°F.
2. Prep a baking sheet with parchment paper.
3. Lightly mash the bananas in a bowl using a fork then go ahead to pour in the chocolate chips, oatmeal and peanut butter. Mix well.
4. Scoop the dough and place the little unbaked cookie on the lined baking sheet. Palm the cookies gently to flatten them.
5. Now bake for about 17 minutes.
6. Transfer to a wire rack and leave to cool.
7. Serve.

Chocolate Chip Brownie Cookie

- Prep time: 5 minutes
- Cooking time: 13 minutes
- Serving: 12
- Classification: Snack
- Age: 2 years and above

INGREDIENTS:

1. All-purpose flour (½ cup)
2. Water (1 tablespoons)
3. Fav brownie mix (1 box)
4. Vegetable oil (6 teaspoons)
5. Peanut butter chips (½ bag)
6. Eggs (2)

INSTRUCTIONS:

1. Prep oven by preheating to 350°F.
2. Pour all the ingredients into a large bowl and mix thoroughly.
3. Coat a baking sheet with butter or nonstick cooking spray.
4. Scoop the cookie dough onto the sheet and slide into the oven to bake for 13 minutes.

Chapter Fourteen: Kiddies Candy

Kids live for the treats and even though they shouldn't binge on sweets whenever they like because too much is bad, they should be allowed to indulge every once in a while. Why not make the candy they consume so you can totally vouch for most of its contents? It's totally easy, I'll show you. That being said, when I say kid, you say candy!

Toffee Crunch Candy

- Prep time: 3 minutes
- Cooking time: 10 minutes
- Serving: 6
- Classification: Snack
- Age: 2 years and above

INGREDIENTS:

1. Water (½ cup)
2. Sugar (2 cups)
3. Baking soda (1 ½ tablespoons)
4. Dark corn syrup (½ cup)

INSTRUCTIONS:

1. First of all, the pot you'll be using has to be pretty big because baking soda needs a lot of room to foam.
2. Prep a fairly sized baking dish (I used 13x9) by coating with aluminum foil that has been lightly greased.
3. Pour the corn syrup, water and sugar into the large pot set over medium heat. Don't stir, just leave it to boil until it gets to 300°F (Check with a candy thermometer) or just get a teaspoon of the mixture and put it in cold water, if it pretty much turns to glass (Not exactly glass because that would be ridiculous), you're on track.
4. Now turn off the heat and add baking soda. Don't stand close to the pot when you do this or you might burn yourself. Keep your kids far away from the kitchen for safety.
5. Stir and transfer the mix to the lined baking dish.
6. Leave it to cool before cutting into pieces.
7. Store in a Ziplock bag and serve whenever you need to.

Homemade Gummy Shapes

- Prep time: 23 minutes
- Cooking time: 7 minutes
- Serving: 12
- Classification: Snack
- Age: 3 years and above

INGREDIENTS:

1. Unflavoured gelatin (2 ¼ oz)
2. Ice cube trays or candy moulds
3. Flavoured gelatin (1 box)
4. Water (⅓ cup)

INSTRUCTIONS:

1. Pour water into a saucepan.
2. Add unflavoured and flavored gelatin and just leave it to sit for about 5 minutes.
3. Place the saucepan over medium heat for 2 minutes to mix the gelatin and water.
4. Transfer mixture to ice cube trays or candy moulds.
5. Leave for 20 minutes to set.
6. Store until ready to serve.

Tiger Fudge

- Prep time: 2 hours 10 minutes
- Cooking time: 15 minutes
- Serving: 12
- Classification: Snack
- Age: 2 years and above

INGREDIENT:

1. Semi-sweet chocolate chips (1 ¼ cups)
2. White chocolate chips (1 ¼ cups)
3. Crunchy peanut butter (1 ⅓ cups)

INSTRUCTIONS:

1. Line an 8x8 pan with aluminum foil coated with nonstick cooking spray.
2. Microwave the white chocolate and a cup of peanut butter then set aside.
3. Do the same to the semi-sweet chocolate and ⅓ cup of peanut butter, but in a different bowl.
4. Scoop some of the white chocolate mixture and drop onto the pan, do the same to the semi-sweet chocolate mixture but on top of the white chocolate mix.
5. Use a knife to twirl through the pan to create beautiful swirls of white and brown.
6. Freeze for 2 hours to set.
7. Take it out of the freezer and cut it into kid size bits.
8. Store in the refrigerator or serve.

Rocky Road Candy

- Prep time: 10 minutes
- Cooking time: 15 minutes
- Serving: 15
- Classification: Snack
- Age: 3 years and above

INGREDIENTS:

1. Mini marshmallows (2 cups)
2. Chopped dark chocolate (1.25 cups)
3. Chopped toasted walnuts (½ cup)

INSTRUCTIONS:

1. Prep a baking sheet by wrapping it in parchment paper.
2. Put the chocolate in a microwave safe bowl and heat in a microwave until it melts. Bring it out and stir.
3. Throw in the marshmallows and chopped walnuts and stir.
4. Scoop and drop spoonfuls onto the baking sheet.
5. Put in the freezer to set and store.

Chocolate Oatmeal No-bake Candy

- Prep time: 5 minutes
- Cooking time: 10 minutes
- Serving: 12
- Classification: Snack
- Age: 2 years and above

INGREDIENTS:

1. Pure maple syrup (¼ cup)
2. Vanilla extract (½ teaspoon)
3. Peanut butter (¼ cup)
4. Salt (¼ teaspoon)
5. Coconut oil (¼ cup)
6. Quick oats (2 cups)
7. Cocoa powder (¼ cup)

INSTRUCTIONS:

1. Prep an 8-inch square pan by lining with parchment paper.
2. Stir the peanut butter, coconut oil and maple syrups over low heat until everything is all mixed up.
3. Now stir in salt, vanilla extract, cocoa powder and oats until you get a smooth mixture.
4. Pour the mixture into the lined pan and press down hard.
5. Put the pan in the freezer to set and store.

Healthy Mound Bars

- Prep time: 30 minutes
- Cooking time: 0 minutes
- Serving: 12
- Classification: Snack
- Age: 2 years and above

INGREDIENTS:

1. Maple syrup (4 tablespoons)
2. Vanilla extract (½ teaspoon)
3. Shredded coconut (1 cup)
4. Coconut oil (2 tablespoons)
5. Cocoa powder (¼ cup)
6. Coconut oil (¼ cup)
7. Salt (⅛ teaspoon)
8. Stevia drops (1 ½ teaspoon)

INSTRUCTIONS:

1. Mix the shredded coconut, maple syrup, coconut oil, vanilla extract and salt in a blender and blitz.
2. Pour the mixture into muffin cups and press it in really well with your hands.
3. Put the muffin cups in the freezer to set for 25 minutes.
4. While that is going on, prepare the chocolate coating. Pour the cocoa powder, coconut oil and stevia drops in a bowl. Mix thoroughly. That's it!
5. Your treats should be hardened now so bring them out of the freezer and put them on a tray lined with parchment paper. Drizzle the chocolate sauce all over them and put them back in the freezer.
6. Serve.

No-sugar Chocolate Fudge

- Prep time: 3 minutes
- Cooking time: 0 minutes
- Serving: 12
- Classification: Snack
- Age: 2 years and above

INGREDIENTS:

1. Overripe banana (1 finger)
2. Pure honey (2 tablespoons)
3. Coconut butter (½ cup)
4. Salt (⅛ teaspoon)
5. Cocoa powder (¼ cup)
6. Vanilla extract (½ teaspoon) This is optional.
7. Cinnamon powder (½ teaspoon)

INSTRUCTIONS:

1. Melt the coconut butter before you start.
2. Mix everything in a blender and pour into a candy mould or ice tray.
3. Put in the freezer to set or for storage.
4. Let it thaw for about 20 minutes before serving.

Peanut Butter Fudge

- Prep time: 5 minutes
- Cooking time: 5 minutes
- Serving: 12
- Classification: Snack
- Age: 2 years and older

INGREDIENTS:

1. Vanilla (1 teaspoon)
2. Butter (1 ¼ cup)
3. Granulated sugar (1 pound)
4. Peanut butter (1 cup)

INSTRUCTIONS:

1. Put peanut butter and 1 cup of butter in a microwave safe dish and heat in the microwave for 2 minutes.
2. Now stir and microwave again for 2 extra minutes.
3. Stir in granulated sugar and vanilla extract and mix thoroughly.
4. Pour mixture into a pan lined with parchment paper and cover the top with another parchment paper.
5. Put in the freezer to set.
6. Cut into kid sizes and store in a Ziplock bag in the fridge.

Chocolate Peanut Butter Chip Fudge

- Prep time: 2 hours
- Cooking time: 5 minutes
- Serving: 12
- Classification: Snack
- Age: 2 years and above

INGREDIENTS:

1. Sweetened condensed milk (1 can)
2. Salt
3. Hershey's semi-sweet chocolate chips (2 cups)
4. Reese's peanut butter chips (1 cup)
5. Vanilla extract (1 teaspoon)

INSTRUCTIONS:

1. Prep an 8-inch square pan by lining with foil.
2. Melt chips in a saucepan over the heat. Add vanilla, salt and condensed milk. Stir until everything is all mixed up and smooth.
3. Turn off the heat and throw in the peanut butter chips. Stir to distribute chips.
4. Pour mixture into prepared pan.
5. Place pan in the freezer to set for 2 hours.
6. It should be all set now, take the solid mixture out of the pan and cut into squares. Make sure you get rid of all the pieces of foil that might have stuck to the candy before you cut.

Chocolate Orange Fudge

- Prep time: 2 hours
- Cooking time: 10 minutes
- Serving: 2 ½ pounds
- Classification: Snack
- Age: 2 years and above

INGREDIENTS:

1. Grated orange peel (2 teaspoons)
2. Sweetened condensed milk (1 can)
3. Semi-sweet chocolate chips (2 ½ cups)
4. Chopped toasted pecans (½ cup)

INSTRUCTIONS:

1. Prep a baking pan by lining with aluminum foil and set aside.
2. Put the chocolate chips and condensed milk in a microwave safe bowl and heat until the chips are completed melted. Remove from the microwave and stir.
3. Add the orange peel and chopped pecans. Stir to distribute.
4. Transfer mix to the prepared baking pan and freeze to set.
5. Remove from the pan and cut into kid sizes and maybe a few adult sizes because we deserve some candy love too.

Chapter Fifteen: Kiddies Juices

Kids are picky and they definitely do not like veggies or anything green really and that's where the nutrients are. We know it, they don't. Juices are like the Trojan Horse of the baby world. You get to sneak in whatever you want, whatever they need and they won't even know it. Some might be able to tell after the last gulp, but ha-ha, it will be too late!

Kids absolutely love juices and smoothies so we can use that to our advantage. You can't blame us; we want the best for our babies. Try out these healthy combos and watch your kids fall in love with you all over again.

Watermelon And Strawberry Drink

- Prep time: 20 minutes
- Cooking time: 0 minutes
- Serving: 2
- Classification: Beverage
- Age: 9 months and above

INGREDIENTS:

1. White sugar (1 cup)
2. Cubed watermelon, seeded (8 cubes)
3. Fresh lemon juice (½ cup)
4. Water (2 cups)
5. Fresh halved strawberries (1 cup)

INSTRUCTIONS:

1. This is super easy. Put the strawberries, sugar, cubed watermelons, lemon juice and water in an electric blender and pulse until you reach the desired consistency.
2. Serve.

Banana Bonkers

- Prep time: 20 minutes
- Cooking time: 0 minutes
- Serving: 3
- Classification: Beverage
- Age: 12 months and above

INGREDIENTS:

1. Lemon sherbet (2 cups)
2. Banana (3 fingers)
3. Crushed ice (1 cup)
4. Fresh grapefruit juice (3 cups)

INSTRUCTIONS:

1. Throw the bananas in an electric blender. You can dice them beforehand to make blending easier. Pulse until it's smooth enough.
2. Add lemon sherbet, crushed ice and grapefruit juice, pulse once and that's pretty much it.
3. Serve.

Oatmeal Shake

- Prep time: 2 hours 10 minutes
- Cooking time: 0 minutes
- Serving: 2
- Classification: Beverage
- Age: 12 months and above

INGREDIENTS:

1. Flaxseed meal (1 tablespoon)
2. Banana (1 finger)
3. Frozen blueberries (1 cup)
4. Rolled oats (¼ cup)
5. Buttermilk (1 cup)
6. Raspberry yogurt (1 cup)
7. Whole almonds (16)
8. Concord grape juice (¼ cup)

INSTRUCTIONS :

1. Remove the skin of the banana and chop into bits. Freeze banana bits for 2 hours.
2. Put the oats, flaxseed meal and almonds in a blender. Blitz until smooth before adding the frozen banana bits, yogurt, buttermilk, grape juice and frozen blueberries. Blitz again until it's smooth enough.

Easy Green Monster Smoothie

- Prep time: 10 minutes
- Cooking time: 0 minutes
- Serving: 4
- Classification: Beverage
- Age: 9 months and above

INGREDIENTS:

1. Chopped skinless and coreless apples (2 small sizes)
2. Orange juice (1 cup)
3. Baby spinach (2 cups)
4. Chopped carrots (1 cup)
5. Fresh strawberries (1 cup)
6. Slices bananas (2 fingers)
7. Ice (1 cup)

INSTRUCTIONS:

1. Pour everything except ice into a blender and puree until it's smooth enough.
2. Pour into glasses and drop some blocks of ice in each glass.
3. Serve.

Fruity Magic

- Prep time: 10 minutes
- Cooking time: 0 minutes
- Serving: 2
- Classification: Beverage
- Age: 12 months and above

INGREDIENTS:

1. Water (½ cup)
2. Chopped banana (1 finger)
3. Nonfat vanilla yogurt (½ cup)
4. Nonfat powdered milk (½ cup)
5. Raspberries (¼ cup)
6. Honey (1 tablespoon)
7. Blackberries (¼ cup)
8. Strawberries, sliced (½ cup)
9. Blueberries (¼ cup)
10. Crushed ice (1 cup)
11. Vanilla whey protein powder (2 spoonfuls)
12. Turbinado sugar (3 tablespoons)

INSTRUCTIONS:

1. Pour everything except crushed ice, honey and sugar in a blender and blitz until super smooth.
2. Pour into glasses and add the rest of the ingredients. Stir to mix.
3. Serve.

Berry Blast Smoothie

- Prep time: 5 minutes
- Cooking time: 0 minutes
- Serving: 3
- Classification: Beverage
- Age: 12 months and above

INGREDIENTS:

1. Strawberry flavored yogurt (1 cup)
2. Milk (1 cup)
3. White sugar (½ teaspoon)
4. Frozen mixed berries (2 cups)
5. Sliced banana (1 finger)

INSTRUCTIONS:

1. Pour all the ingredients into an electric blender and pulse until it's smooth enough.
2. Add more water for a thinner consistency.
3. Serve fresh.

Avocado And Blueberry Smoothie

- Prep time: 5 minutes
- Cooking time:
- Serving: 2 cups
- Classification: Beverages
- Age: 9 months and above

INGREDIENTS:

1. Plain Greek yogurt (1 container)
2. Water (½ cup)
3. Frozen blueberries (1 cup)
4. Diced avocado (¼ small size)
5. Almond milk (½ cup)

INSTRUCTIONS:

1. Put everything into a blender and pulse until it's all mixed up and smooth. Told you? Easy peasy.
2. Serve with ice or not.

Orange Cream Sycle Smoothie

- Prep time: 3 hours 5 minutes
- Cooking time: 0 minutes
- Serving: 2
- Classification: Main meal, beverage
- Age: 12 months

INGREDIENTS:

1. Frozen pineapple bits (½ cup)
2. Honey (1 tablespoon)
3. Mandarin oranges + juice (1 can)
4. Vanilla soymilk (1 cup)
5. Vanilla flavoured yogurt (½ cup)

INSTRUCTIONS:

1. Drain the can of oranges and put the oranges in a Ziplock bag to freeze.
2. Now put the frozen pineapple bits and frozen oranges in a blender first. Add every other ingredient and pulse until it starts to look like a milkshake.
3. Throw in more ice if you want and blend.
4. Serve.

Lemonade

- Prep time: 20 minutes
- Cooking time: 5 minutes
- Serving: 6
- Classification: Beverage
- Age: 2 years and above

INGREDIENTS:

1. Cold water (6 cups)
2. Granulated sugar (1 cups)
3. Organic lemons (8 large size)

INSTRUCTIONS:

1. Pour 1 cup of water in a saucepan set over medium heat. Add sugar and stir until all the sugar disappears.
2. Turn off the heat, transfer the syrup to a bowl and place it in the fridge.
3. Get the juice out of the fresh lemons into a bowl. Add the remaining cold water and stir.
4. Pour the now cold syrup into the lemon water and stir to mix.
5. Decorate with lemon slices or mint leaves if you like.
6. Enjoy!

Frozen Strawberry And Lemonade Smoothie

- Prep time: 5 minutes
- Cooking time: 0 minutes
- Serving: 2
- Classification: Beverages
- Age: 2 years and above

INGREDIENTS:

1. Water (¼ cup)
2. Swerve natural sweetener (½ cup)
3. Lemon juice (½ cup)
4. Lemon liquid Stevia (1 teaspoon)
5. Ice (2 cups)
6. Strawberries (½
7. Salt

INSTRUCTIONS:

1. Pour the sweeteners, water and lemon juice into a blender.
2. Wash the strawberries, cut off the stem and throw them in the blender.
3. Pulse twice and add ice.
4. Pulse until you get a slightly thick mixture. Add more sweetener if you like and pulse again.
5. Serve.

Mango Mocktail

- Prep time: 5 minutes
- Cooking time: 0 minutes
- Serving: 2
- Classification: Beverages
- Age: 2 years and above

INGREDIENTS:

1. Vanilla extract (1 teaspoon)
2. Frozen mango juice (1 cup)
3. Sugar (2 tablespoons)
4. Milk (2 oz)
5. Vanilla ice cream (1 scoop)

INSTRUCTIONS:

1. Put all ingredients into the blender and pulse until it is smooth and all mixed up.
2. Serve with ice.

Cookie Milkshake

- Prep time: 10 minutes
- Cooking time: 0 minutes
- Serving: 1
- Classification: Beverages
- Age: 2 years and above

INGREDIENTS:

1. Whole milk (8 oz)
2. Any flavor of ice cream (16 oz)
3. Cookies (8 small sizes)
4. Sprinkles (Optional)

5. Caramel fudge (Optional)
6. Whipped cream (Optional)
7. Strawberries (Optional)
8. Chocolate fudge (Optional)
9. Bananas (Optional)
10. Cherries (Optional)

INSTRUCTIONS:

1. Pour the ice cream and whole milk in a blender and pulse twice.
2. Throw in the cookies and pulse until it reaches a certain consistency you'd like.
3. Pour mixture into a glass.
4. This is the time to add any of the optional ingredients if you happen to be using any of them.
5. Crush some extra cookies for toppings.
6. Serve and enjoy!

Conclusion

Healthy eating habits are essential for proper child development. Starting off the day with a nutrient packed meal will give your baby the energy boost they'll need to run around all day seeing as that particular activity makes up the bulk of their day. There are so many more recipes for babies and toddlers on the Web, so feel free to look them up if you have exhausted all the amazing recipes in this book. Your children are your priority. If you don't feed them, who will?

Sending you love and light!

Printed in Great
Britain
by Amazon